DATE DUE

JUN 0 9 2005			
JUL 1 1 2005			
AUG 0 8 2005			
8/29			
SEP 0 6 2005			
SEP 2 7 2005			
JAN 1 8 2007			

DEMCO 38-296

Lily Quench

and the Search for King Dragon

Lily Quench

and the Search for King Dragon

NATALIE JANE PRIOR

Illustrations by Janine Dawson

PUFFIN BOOKS

Visit Lily's Web site at
www.lilyquench.com

PUFFIN BOOKS
Published by the Penguin Group
Penguin Young Readers Group, 345 Hudson Street, New York, New York 10014, U.S.A.
Penguin Group (Canada), 10 Alcorn Avenue, Toronto, Ontario, Canada M4V 3B2
(a division of Pearson Penguin Canada Inc.)
Penguin Books Ltd, 80 Strand, London WC2R 0RL, England
Penguin Ireland, 25 St Stephen's Green, Dublin 2, Ireland
(a division of Penguin Books Ltd)
Penguin Group (Australia), 250 Camberwell Road, Camberwell, Victoria 3124, Australia
(a division of Pearson Australia Group Pty Ltd)
Penguin Books India Pvt Ltd, 11 Community Centre, Panchsheel Park,
New Delhi—110 017, India
Penguin Group (NZ), Cnr Airborne and Rosedale Roads, Albany, Auckland,
New Zealand (a division of Pearson New Zealand Ltd)
Penguin Books (South Africa) (Pty) Ltd, 24 Sturdee Avenue, Rosebank, Johannesburg
2196, South Africa

Registered Offices: Penguin Books Ltd, 80 Strand, London WC2R 0RL, England

First published in Australia and New Zealand by Hodder Headline Australia Pty Limited
(A member of the Hodder Headline Group), 2004
Published by Puffin Books, a division of Penguin Young Readers Group, 2005

1 3 5 7 9 10 8 6 4 2

Puffin Books ISBN 0-14-240267-2

Printed in the United States of America

This book is dedicated to Belinda Bolliger and Romina Chapnik, who always believed in Lily and never failed her.

Thanks, Belinda and Romina.

Lily couldn't have had a kinder publisher or a more tireless editor.

Some Old Friends . . .

Lily Quench

Last of the dragon-slaying Quenches of Ashby, Lily drove the Black Count's army out of Ashby and restored King Lionel to his throne. Lily later rediscovered her family's secret weapon (metal-eating Quenching Drops), discovered the Treasure of Mote Ely, and tracked down the magical Eye Stones to prevent them from being used in an invasion from the Black Empire.

Queen Dragon

Sinhault Fierdaze (known to her friends as Queen Dragon) is a three-thousand-year-old crimson dragon, the size of a four-story house.

King Lionel of Ashby

The son of King Alwyn the Last, who was killed at the Siege of Ashby during the Black Count's invasion.

Queen Evangeline of Ashby

A former supporter of the Black Count, Evangeline helped drive the count's forces from Ashby and later married the king.

Crystal Bright

Queen Evangeline's shifty mother, Crystal, used to work for the Black Count and still complains that things in Ashby have never been the same since the Black Squads left. She worked briefly as a spy for General Sark.

Mr. Trevor Hartley

The minister of the Ashby Church. Mr. Hartley helped Lily restore the lost prince, Lionel, to the throne of Ashby.

Dr. Angela Hartley

A former slave of the Black Count, Angela was the foster mother of his son, Gordon, for many years. She has returned to live and work in Ashby.

Murdo

Born in the past, Murdo joined Gordon's army at the Castle of Mote Ely, and was feared as a cruel bully. He was brought forward into Lily's time so his life could be saved after an accident.

Gordon, the Black Count

The only son of the Black Count, Gordon lost his empire to the treachery of his father's friend, General Sark. He disappeared into the past through a magical Eye Stone in the Black Mountains.

Manuelo

A mysterious cloaked fighter from the Black Mountains, Manuelo tried to steal the Treasure of Mote Ely from the vaults of Ashby Castle. Nobody knows his true identity.

King Dragon

Thousands of years ago, during the Great War of the Dragons, Queen Dragon's long-lost fiancé led a small party of dragons through an Eye Stone and disappeared.

Veronica

Gordon's former lieutenant from Mote Ely Castle, and Murdo's sister.

Patterson

A shifty character from the Black Mountains, who has become close friends with Crystal.

General Sark

Ruler of the Black Empire, and usurper of the Black Count's power.

Aunt Cassy and Roger

Evil magicians who are thousands of years old. They need dragon's blood to stay alive.

Jason Pearl

Son of the Keeper of Ashby Thicket, Jason was promoted to Royal Chamberlain after helping King Lionel return to Ashby.

Wilibald Zouche

The former ruler of Ashby for the Black Count, Sir Wilibald Zouche is now a member of the Royal Council.

Annacondea's Eyrie
King Dragon's Cave
Here Lily & Queen Dragon arrived in Eydelen
Eydelen
Valley of the Dragons
Roger & Cassy's Camp

chapter one

The Fall of the Citadel

The smell of cordite drifted on the winter air. There were screams, explosions, the flurry of snowflakes. Machine guns rattled on the ramparts of the Black Citadel, and dragonets buzzed overhead. Above the din, the air was filled with the sound of people dying. The snow in the citadel courtyard was stained with fresh blood and scented with human fear.

General Sark, Supreme Commander of All the Armies, Lord of the Citadel, ruler of the Black Empire, stood in the western watchtower looking anxiously into the rapidly falling dusk. He was waiting for reinforcements. The attack had come unexpectedly three nights before, when the miners had blasted their way into the citadel cellars. They had been working away quietly for weeks and, once they were in, had quickly overrun the lower levels. Sark could not believe how many there were of them. It had not occurred to him that if someone managed to rally the miners, they would be a threat. Now that someone had come—a mysterious freedom fighter called Manuelo. In the battle for the citadel, Manuelo had seemed to be everywhere: on the ramparts, in the corridors, in the courtyard of the citadel, his distinctive black cloak flaring around him as he urged his followers on. Now, after three days of fighting, the miners controlled all the citadel except the Great Courtyard itself.

"There's no sign of Brigadier Miller, sir," said the young captain who had accompanied Sark to the watchtower. "Manuelo must have secured the passes. That's what I would do in his place." Brigadier Miller had been putting down a rebellion in the foothills of the Black Mountains. His Eastern Brigade had been the closest troops available.

"Dangerous work, sir, mobilizing troops in winter," said the watchtower guard helpfully. "Avalanches, blizzards. There's lots of things can go wrong."

"Nobody asked for your opinion." Sark's voice was as icy as the wind off the peaks. Right now, he did not care whether half the Eastern Brigade froze to death along the way, provided the other half remained to fight for him when they finally came. The guard saluted, but the young captain was not so easily put off.

"In any case, sir, they're not going to get here before nightfall." He looked the general squarely in the eye. "I know it's not my place, sir, but without aid, the citadel will fall within the next couple of hours."

"I will not surrender to a pack of stinking miners and a rabble-rouser in a cloak," snapped Sark. "If I was not so short of officers, I would shoot you where you stand for that remark." He took one last look out into the gathering dusk. "Carry on," he said curtly. The guards clicked their heels, and the general swept down the stairs, his greatcoat swirling around his ankles.

In the Great Courtyard, the situation was

clearly desperate. The last of the general's troops had fallen back toward the gatehouse and the armories, and white flags with a red fist—the Hand of Manuelo—were already flying from some of the battlements. Sark saw a young woman in miner's overalls scaling one of the curtain walls with a banner tied around her waist. He drew his pistol and fired at her, but missed. The miner lost her balance and fell into the crowd. Sark hurried on, but when he looked back a few minutes later, the flag was draped from the battlements, the red fist glowing against its white background like blood on snow.

"I shall not let this empire go without a fight!" he roared. "To me, soldiers! To me!" The rallying cry went raggedly up around the courtyard. On the battlements, Sark could hear the miners singing their wretched chant about the Hand of Manuelo as they hurled chunks of broken masonry at the retreating Black Squads. He even glimpsed Manuelo himself in his black cloak, urging the main body of his followers on. A good shot would have picked him off, but it was as if he was somehow untouchable. *Perhaps*, thought Sark fleetingly, *it was because Manuelo didn't even seem to care what happened to himself.*

"Manuelo! Manuelo! Manuelo!" shouted the miners. A few calls of *"Sark forever!"* went up from his own followers, but most of the Black Squads were too busy running away to be bothered.

"Regroup!" Sark shouted. He ran several steps up a flight of stone stairs. "Regroup around the armory!" His exhausted captains were rallying their men as best they could, when against all hope a shout came from the watchtower above them.

"Reinforcements!"

"It's Brigadier Miller!" shouted the young captain. His weary face lit up. "Brigadier Miller! The Eastern Brigade has arrived!"

"Open the gates!" roared Sark. "Open the gates!"

Ragged cheers went up from the exhausted troops, and there was a general surge toward the gatehouse. Half a dozen troopers threw off the great metal bar that secured the gates, and another grabbed the lever that controlled them. An ancient motor ground into life somewhere beneath the flagstones. The portcullis went up, and the gates swung slowly inward.

Black Squad troops swarmed into the citadel,

wallowing through filthy, bloodstained snow. Tanks roared up the road behind them, driving three abreast through the enormous gateway. From his viewpoint on the stairs, Sark heard his troops' cheers turn to cries of dismay. He looked up. There, his head protruding from the dome of a tank, was a familiar figure in a black cloak.

"What witchcraft is this?" screamed Sark. He whirled around to where he had seen Manuelo on the battlements only a minute before, but he had vanished. The tank carrying the cloaked figure roared past him to the very center of the citadel courtyard. At the sight of Manuelo, the miners burst into cheers of triumph. Tears ran down their bloodstained, dirty faces, and they waved their jackhammers and shovels above their heads.

The Eastern Brigade had joined forces with Manuelo. The day was lost. Worn out, outnumbered, and with nowhere to retreat to, the defending troops started throwing down their weapons. Sark stood for a moment, staring at the cloaked figure on the tank. Suddenly his nerve broke, and he turned and fled.

"Manuelo! Manuelo! Manuelo!"

"Gordon! Gordon! Gordon!"

In a trice the general's emblem disappeared from the top of the gatehouse. A white flag with a huge red fist on it was raised above the tower. Another smaller one swiftly followed it. It was black with a twisted rope on it, the flag of the Black Counts who, for the last two hundred years, had held the Black Mountains in thrall.

The Black Count, Gordon, had returned to claim his inheritance.

chapter two

News from the Empire

Footsteps ran along the corridors of Ashby Castle, *click, click, click*, against the polished floors. The Royal Chamberlain, Sir Jason Pearl, was in a hurry, and as he ran, servants, visitors, and castle residents fell back or jumped out of his way. The chamberlain dashed out of the main doors and crossed the bailey to the South Tower. He ran up its spiral staircase, past the refurbished library and the king's private sitting room, and stopped at a door with a small heart cut in the honey-colored wood.

"Your Majesty!" Jason banged on the door

with his staff of office. *"Your Majesty!"*

The door opened, and King Lionel's head popped out. There were nappy pins in his sweater and something white and streaky on his shoulder.

"For goodness' sake, Jason!" hissed the king. "We've only just got the baby off to sleep!"

"Sorry." Jason wrinkled his nose at the king's sweater. "I didn't mean to, only—it's very important! I thought you'd want to know as soon as possible. We've just had news by pigeon. The Black Citadel has fallen!"

Lionel's breath hissed. "Fallen?"

"It's only a short note." Breathlessly, Jason pulled the coiled strip of paper from his pocket and pressed it into the king's outstretched hand. Queen Evangeline appeared at her husband's shoulder, and together they read the tiny scroll. In tiny, neat handwriting, it said that the Black Citadel had fallen, that the rebel leader Manuelo was in command, and that the Black Army had surrendered to his complete control. General Sark was missing in action. The note was signed Trevor and Angela Hartley, and there was a P.S.: *More news follows very shortly.*

Lionel crumpled the note and thrust it into his

pocket. "I had no idea this was coming. We've got to tell Lily! Quickly!"

The king started running up the stairs. With a backward glance to ensure that the baby Princess Elizabeth was safe in the charge of her nurse, the queen followed. They reached the top of the stairs in double quick time, and the king flung open a narrow door in the stone wall. A blast of cold air blew in from the ramparts. As the king and queen emerged, a huge red bulk launched itself over the opposite set of battlements.

"Queen Dragon!" Lionel shouted. "Lily! Come back! It's an emergency!" He waved his arms like a windmill and ran along the battlements. But Queen Dragon did not look back. She had already banked to starboard and was sailing off into the eastern sky like a gigantic red-sailed galleon. As the king reached the end of the ramparts, she flew into a bank of cloud and disappeared.

High above the ocean, winging her way to the island of Skansey, Lily Quench was thinking of King Dragon.

It was cold, the clouds brushed wetly against

her face and hands, and her fireproof cape was wrapped tightly around her shoulders. Lily was in a pensive and melancholy mood. In her heart, she knew that this search for Queen Dragon's lost fiancé, the mysterious King Dragon, might well be their last adventure together. In a vision, King Dragon had told Lily that the time had come for Queen Dragon to rejoin him, and Lily knew that she owed it to Queen Dragon to help her find him. Since they had become friends, Queen Dragon had helped her many times. In the frozen wastes of Dragon's Downfall, they had tracked down the blue lily to make the Quenching Drops that would repel King Lionel's enemies. They had traveled through time and passed through unimaginable peril to close off the Eye Stones, the magical passages through time that those same enemies planned to use. Never once had Queen Dragon protested or held back from the danger. She had done it all out of love. Now, Lily knew, it was time for her to repay that debt.

"I have to go," Lily had explained to the king and queen when she had taken leave of them earlier that morning. "I swore to Queen Dragon that I would help her. For thousands of years, she has dreamed of rejoining King Dragon. Now we have a chance of finding him. We have closed off most of the Eye Stones. Ashby is as secure as we can make it. I promise you, I will come back as soon as I can."

"I know you will," Lionel had answered. "But I am sorry for it, Lily, all the same. You will forgive me for being selfish, but having Queen Dragon fight for us has been more helpful than I could say. I had hoped . . . Well. You know what I hoped for, but in the end I can only tell you how I feel. It's a grievous thing to be letting Queen Dragon go."

"I try not to think about it," said Lily honestly. "I do not want to lose her either. But I know in my heart that this is the right thing to do."

Lionel sighed. "I wish I could be so sure. No one has seen King Dragon since the Great War of the Dragons, and that was thousands of years ago. Do you really believe you will find him?"

"Our friends the Hartleys were separated for over ten years," Lily reminded him. "Angela was a slave in the Black Mountains. Yet in the end, they got their miracle. Why should there not be one for Queen Dragon as well?"

"A dragon-sized miracle," said Lionel. "Well, if it's meant to be this way, then maybe there will be one."

"It's what I'm hoping for," Lily had answered. She had not said what she thought: that it was what she was afraid of, too.

They started going down over the ocean. Lily saw Queen Dragon's volcano, where she lived in an underground cavern, and beyond it, a sprinkling of tiny green islands. The nearest and largest was Skansey, where Lily had a little house. It had been built by an old man called Daniel who had once been Queen Dragon's friend; he had planted an apple orchard and farmed the sheep that still roamed, half wild, over the island. Lily had never bothered with the sheep, but she did love the apple trees with their gnarled trunks, and enjoyed eating their fruit when it was in season. Ashby was her home, but Skansey was her refuge. It was her own private place where only she and Queen Dragon could go.

"What was that?" A plume of smoke seemed to be rising from the island, but as Lily craned forward to see, a puff of cloud got in the way.

Queen Dragon sniffed and started going down more steeply.

"I don't know," she said. "I can smell smoke though."

They emerged from the cloud bank and flew down toward the beach. Now Lily could see clearly the thin line of black smoke that rose from the sheltered hollow where her house was. Both she and Queen Dragon went very quiet. Queen Dragon pulled in her wings and landed on the sand.

Lily scrambled down from her head and ran up the beach. The stink of smoke floated toward her, and, as she crested the dunes, she almost fell over a dead sheep, charred black and lying in the grass. Lily gave a strangled cry and started running down the hill.

"Lily, be careful!" Queen Dragon called out a warning, but Lily did not—could not—stop. For she had already seen where the smoke was coming from. It was her house, or what was left of it, and the splintered, burned remains of her beloved orchard.

Skansey had been pillaged and despoiled.

In far-off Ashby Water, night had fallen. The king and queen were eating dinner in their private rooms. Though neither admitted it, after the morning's drama, they were both feeling tired and distinctly flat.

"What do you think is going to happen?" asked Evangeline as she picked over her shepherd's pie.

"I don't know." Lionel's face was drawn; even the prospect of caramel tart for dessert couldn't lift his spirits. He looked at Elizabeth sleeping in her pram beside their table, and thought how perfect she was with her pursed lips and the long eyelashes tickling her rosebud cheeks. The princess's birth had changed everything, both for her parents and for Ashby. Lionel was used to uncertainty and danger, but now that he was a father he also felt frightened. He did not want Elizabeth to grow up the way he had himself, alone and in exile, without a home or family, with the horrible memory of what had happened to his father always hanging over him.

He put his knife and fork down on his plate. Outside, in the rain and cold, a peculiar buzzing noise could be heard growing closer and louder, as if something was traveling toward them. Lionel and Evangeline looked at each other. The noise grew even louder and approached until it was directly overhead. They heard shouts and running feet in the bailey, and then the baby at Lionel's side woke up and began to cry.

"That sounds like a dragonet." Lionel pushed back his chair. Evangeline picked up Elizabeth and tried to comfort her, but the noise was by now so loud she screamed harder than ever. Bright lights shone through the window, and they caught a glimpse of something large and dark going down in the bailey. Lionel bounded across to the window and looked out. "It *is* a dragonet!"

The queen clutched the princess to her chest. "It's started already! We're being invaded!"

"One dragonet doesn't make an invasion, Evie." Lionel grabbed his shoes and started pulling them on over his socks. "Wait here with Elizabeth. I'm going to go and see who it is."

He hurried down the stairs and out into the bailey. The dragonet was standing black and alone on the cobblestones, already surrounded by a ring of Royal Guards. Stinking puffs of black smoke emerged from its exhaust, but as Lionel emerged from the tower the pilot killed the engine and everything shuddered into silence. The cockpit door opened, and the dragonet's sole occupant, a bullet-headed man in a black greatcoat, slowly stood up with his hands above his head.

"Asylum!" he croaked. "I come seeking asylum!"

"Who are you?" Lionel pushed through the crowded ring of guards. He had never seen the man before, but from the masses of silver braid on his epaulettes he was clearly someone important. "I am King Lionel of Ashby. If you are seeking asylum, I demand to know who you are!"

"Sark," said the man. "I'm General Sark of the Black Empire. And if you're wise you're going to listen to what I have to say!"

chapter three

The Pillaging of Skansey

Lily stood looking at her ruined house and garden, tears streaming uncontrollably down her face. Hot ash eddied around her, and a burning flake settled on her skin. If the island had been attacked by a dragon, her home could not have been more thoroughly destroyed.

Queen Dragon surveyed the destruction. "Oh, Lily," she said helplessly. "I'm so sorry."

"But how did this happen?" Lily pulled her fireproof cape up over her head and started picking her way through the devastation. The heat struck up from the ground beneath her boots, but it was not as hot as the feeling in her heart. "This must have happened only this morning. Oh, Queen Dragon, I wish we'd never come here!"

There was nothing Queen Dragon could say that would have made Lily feel any better. The destruction of her house was almost total. All that was left of it were a few charred sticks and a wobbly skeleton where the staircase had led up to the bedroom and the apple loft. Lily picked up a half-burned stick and crunched through the cinders in what had been her downstairs room, scraping around helplessly for some sign of her belongings. But there was nothing there: only the twisted metal wreck of the kitchen stove, some half-melted spoons and forks, and a few bits of broken crockery that had obviously fallen out of the dresser as it burned.

Lily picked up part of a teacup. It was one with roses on it, still visible beneath the soot when she wiped it away. She put it carefully into her pocket and went out into the garden, which, if anything, was even more heartbreaking than the house. Spot fires were still burning here and there among the remains of her orchard, and the sweet distinctive scent of smoldering applewood was overpowering. Her vegetable garden was gone, her climbing rosebushes had perished, and the precious patch of blue lilies that she had planted at the beginning of the year had completely vanished, trampled into the earth and covered with ash and cinder. Luckily most of the flowers had already been picked and used to make Quenching Drops, Lily's family's secret weapon, and since the silk bag where she kept the blue lily petals also contained some seed, the lilies could be replanted. But it was the trees, her beautiful apple trees, that upset Lily the most. Not a single sapling remained, and she knew from what Queen Dragon had told her that many of them had been nearly a hundred years old.

A few of the old season's windfalls lay hidden under the ashes where the fire had missed them, brown and mushy from frosts, or scorched black by the flames. The orchard was also dotted with charred sheep carcasses, like the one Lily had found on the sand dune. As she walked through the destruction, it struck Lily that whatever had caused this fire must have moved awfully quickly. The sheep grazing in the orchard had been trapped by flames or overcome by smoke: there had been no time for them to run away. Lily looked up, but the sky was clear and blue. Her first thought, that the blaze had been started by lightning, was beginning to look most unlikely.

Queen Dragon was coming to a similar conclusion.

"Lily," she said, "I think we've got a problem. This isn't one fire. It's several. Look." She pointed with her claw. "The fire has moved outward from this point. But if you look over there, near the house, you can see the same pattern. Here's a third starting point, and a fourth. There's no way four fires could start like this naturally, all at the same time. They must have been deliberately lit."

"But who could have done it?" Lily demanded. "No one else even knows where Skansey is!"

"Obviously someone does know," said Queen Dragon. "An enemy who has come here on purpose. Someone who wanted to prevent your coming to Skansey again—or who wanted to pay you back for something." She hesitated. "We must be careful, Lily. Those fires are still burning, so this damage is very recent."

"You mean, whoever is responsible may still be here on the island?"

"If they were, I would be able to scent them," said Queen Dragon. "No. I mean we have to be careful that whoever it was doesn't come back. Remember the time you were kidnapped?"

"The Eye Stone!" Lily exclaimed. Gordon, the son of the Black Count, had sent his followers through an Eye Stone on nearby Merryweather Hill to capture Lily and take her back to his hideout in the past. The Merryweather Hill Eye Stone was still there, one of the few Lily and Queen Dragon had not closed off.

"If Gordon's still hiding in the past, there are any number of working Eye Stones he can use," Queen Dragon pointed out. "If he's in our own time, there's the one at Dragon's Downfall in the Black Mountains we decided not to destroy. Gordon's your chief enemy, Lily. He *has* to be our main suspect."

"Perhaps." Lily thought a moment. "I don't think so, though. Gordon's obsessed with reclaiming his father's empire, but he's not spiteful. I don't think he'd burn someone's house down just for fun."

"All right. That twerp Murdo, then, who tried to drown you," said Queen Dragon, referring to

Gordon's erstwhile lieutenant. "You can't say *he* isn't spiteful. Or what about that awful old witch, Cassy? She was the one who taught Gordon how to use the Eye Stone in the first place. Then there was her friend, young Rabbit—now *he* was a nasty piece of work. And what about that scary sister of his? What was her name? Vanessa, or Vivian, or—"

"Veronica. Captain Veronica. She was Gordon's second in command." Something seemed to tickle in Lily's head at the mention of Veronica's name, but she let it pass. "Let's not worry about who did it, Queen Dragon. Getting worked up is not going to bring back my orchard. This was probably going to be my last visit to Skansey anyway." She sighed. "I'm just sorry it had to end like this. I'd have liked to be able to remember it the way it was."

"You still can, Lily," said Queen Dragon. "Come on. Let's destroy the Eye Stone on Merryweather Hill, before anyone decides to use it again."

King Lionel of Ashby sat at the head of his Royal Council table, Queen Evangeline at his side. The curtains were drawn, the doors were closed, and

Royal Guards were stationed in the corridor for a secret meeting.

"Now, Sark," said Lionel to the bullet-headed figure sitting opposite him. "Let's get this straight. You've come here asking for my help. Considering the Black Empire is Ashby's biggest enemy, you're going to need to do a lot of convincing."

"I've already told you why I'm here," said Sark. "The Black Citadel has fallen to Manuelo and his rebel miners. If I hadn't fled, they would have killed me."

"Our intelligence has already told us about Manuelo," said Lionel. "As for you, I'm not sure I want you here any more than in the Black Mountains. You'll have to do better than that if you want to stay."

"I've no intention of staying any longer than I have to," said Sark. "I offer you an alliance. I want troops, arms, and assistance so that I can return and throw this interloper out. It is in Ashby's interests that Manuelo should be defeated. If you do not help me, I can guarantee that he and what is left of the Black Army will be knocking on your castle door within weeks."

"How so?" said Lionel.

"Because of this." Sark put a hand into an inner pocket of his uniform and brought out a small black-and-silver velvet pouch. He pushed it across the table to the king. "Go on. Open it. I think you'll understand when you see what's inside."

Lionel reached for the bag and drew it toward him across the tabletop. It was secured by a simple drawstring. The king hesitated, then tipped a flat, round object out into his hand. It was a seal, carved out of a piece of obsidian, the size of a man's palm. On one side was a profile portrait of a man with a cruel face. On the other was a twisted rope, and a motto: *I LIVE TO CONQUER*.

"It is the Black Seal," said Sark. "The imperial seal of the Black Counts. It belonged to Raymond Longshanks, the first of the line—that is his picture on the obverse. No one can become Black Count without it; it must be present at the investiture ceremony as the source and symbol of their power. I am offering it to you as a sign of my good intentions."

"I have no desire whatsoever to rule the Black Empire," said Lionel sharply. "It is a tainted inheritance that has belonged for two hundred years to a line of corrupt and depraved men. So do not think you can tempt me with your talk of alliances. Ashby and its territories are quite enough for me."

"You miss the point, king," said Sark through his teeth. "I do not offer you the seal so you can set yourself up in the Black Count's place. In your hands, as in mine, the Black Seal is nothing; it is powerless without the bloodline to go with it. But he who holds the Black Seal in his keeping has the power to stop the one whose bloodline is tied to that place and that empire, the one who is the Black Count's heir."

Evangeline blanched. "Gordon?"

"His banners were flying alongside Manuelo's when I left the citadel," said Sark. "Gordon has returned to claim his inheritance. If you do not go to him, as soon as he learns you hold the seal, he will come to you. Now, King Lionel of Ashby. Will you talk?"

Up on Merryweather Hill, the surviving sheep stood clustered in a terrified flock around the Eye Stone. Their numbers were rather more depleted than Lily had realized, but it was still a relief to discover that some of them had survived. As Lily and Queen Dragon climbed up the hill toward them, they scattered and ran off, bleating, down the other side.

"Poor things," said Queen Dragon as they disappeared into the gathering dusk. "Year after year they've just stood around eating grass and apples, and then their friends get turned into a barbeque before their eyes. It must have been terrible for them."

"Not as terrible as it was for the ones that got burned alive," said Lily. She walked across the tufty grass to the spot where the Eye Stone had been built, thousands of years before. It appeared harmless enough, like an old wellhead with a red brick coping, overgrown with grass and ferns that had browned off with the onset of the cold weather. It did not look to Lily as if anyone had recently used it. The fern fronds were untrampled, there was no sign of footprints, and, most revealing of all, no telltale smear of dragon's blood on the coping.

"Don't stand too near, Lily," said Queen Dragon. "Let me get it closed off first. Ouch! I wish there was some other way of doing this!" She stuck a claw in between the scales on her left foot and winced as the tears flooded down her cheeks and dropped onto the brickwork. Then, when the Eye Stone was thoroughly wet, she turned around, lifted her enormous tail, and brought it down with a resounding crash.

Queen Dragon swiveled her head around. "Out of order?"

"Out of order," Lily confirmed. Her memory of the night when Gordon's followers had thrown her into the well was fresh enough for her to feel glad that the Eye Stone was gone. All the same, she could not help feeling uneasy about the fact that whoever had started the fires had seemed not to arrive through it.

Lily sat down on the grass, wrapped for warmth in her fireproof cape. She unpacked her picnic supper: ham sandwiches, cheese, and a slice of pineapple upside-down cake. There was no fruit, because she had expected to be eating apples from the orchard. Lily ate the food quickly, hardly tasting it at all. Queen Dragon sat beside her, a warm and comforting presence.

"Do you think King Dragon will come to meet us?" she asked.

"I don't know," Lily admitted. She crumpled

up the paper bag and put it in her pocket. There had been an anxious note in Queen Dragon's voice. She had not spoken much about why they'd come to Skansey, but it was impossible for Lily not to realize how nervous she was. "In my vision he just said if we sat on Merryweather Hill and had faith in our hearts, the door would be opened to those who are meant to come."

"That's what I'm afraid of," said Queen Dragon. "Oh, Lily, suppose I'm not *meant* to go to Eydelen? Suppose King Dragon decides I'm not good enough—"

"That's not what he told me, Queen Dragon," said Lily gently. "If anyone gets left behind, it will probably be me."

Queen Dragon reared up. "That's even worse! Lily, what an awful thought! Of course you have to come with me. Why, when you told me about the vision, I promised you I'd stay with you for as long as you needed. I won't go if you can't come—"

"Queen Dragon, let's not worry about that," said Lily. "The door to Eydelen hasn't even opened. Let's just have a rest and talk about it later." She patted Queen Dragon's claw, and her friend settled down again. Lily spread out a blanket and lay down. Before ten minutes had gone by, she heard gentle dragonish snores and smelled a wisp of smoke from Queen Dragon's nostrils. Worn out from all the flying, Queen Dragon had fallen asleep.

Lily could not sleep. The scent of smoke was still rising up from the orchard at the bottom of the hill, and her heart burned with sadness. Instead, she lay watching the stars appear one by one in the night sky. They were always very bright here on Skansey where the skies were clear and there were no streetlights to mar the view, but tonight her eyes kept drifting to the northern horizon where they seemed to float above the sea.

A whole part of her life was over, and she was starting to realize it. Skansey was gone; Queen Dragon was moving on. It was the start of the end, and there was nothing she could do to stop it. Yet she was still holding on, trying to tell herself it wasn't going to happen, that if she only closed her eyes and wished, she would somehow go back to where she and Queen Dragon had been when they had met. The only problem was that she couldn't. Even an Eye Stone couldn't take her back now, for Lily Quench was a different person from the scared little girl who had confronted Queen Dragon on the scrap heap at the grommet factory. That Lily had disappeared into the past as surely as Gordon had when he had traveled through the Eye Stone at Dragon's Downfall, and nothing she did could ever bring her back.

Lily put her hand in her pocket. Her fingers closed around the broken teacup she had found in the ashes of the house, and she brought it out and looked at it. It had been the only survivor of a set that Captain Zouche's Black Squad had smashed on the day she had met Queen Dragon, and now it, too, was gone. Lily got quietly to her feet and walked across the cold grass to the wellhead. For a moment she stood looking at the pattern of pink rosebuds around the teacup's rim, and then she let the cup fall gently from her fingers into the well.

There was a second or two's silence followed by a soft plunk as it hit the cool, clear water at the bottom. Lily smiled. She went back to Queen Dragon's side and settled down to listen to her gentle breathing. As she drifted into sleep, it seemed to her that the dim stars in the constellation of the dragon looked far brighter than they had before. They rose like a fiery necklace out of the sea. Then the veil of sleep came down across them, and the sound of the sea washing on the shores of the island drew Lily into her dreams.

chapter four

Strange Reunions

Lily woke up to the sound of birdsong.

It was not a sound she was used to hearing. There were no birds in Ashby Water: all the big trees had been cut down under the Black Count's rule, and there was nowhere for them to perch. On Skansey there were only gulls and seabirds. Their cries could scarcely be described as tuneful, so at first Lily thought that the cheerful twittering she heard all around her must be part of a dream. She lay with her eyes closed, hoping it would last a little longer. But the sun had come up and was shining down on her where she lay;

it tickled Lily's eyelids and made her feel uncomfortably hot. She was awake now, truly awake, and the birdsong was still there. If anything, it had become louder.

Lily opened her eyes and sat up. A small bird was sitting on a low branch of a nearby tree, bubbling a song. When she moved, it flew away like a green flash. Lily drew a deep breath and felt air cleaner and clearer than any she had breathed before rush into her lungs. It was no dream, then. It was real, real enough to hear and touch and smell. She was on the cliff top where in her vision she had met King Dragon, sitting on grass so green it looked like a painting, under a sky so blue it took her breath away. It looked like the clearest and lightest of sapphires held up to sunlight, or a crystal ocean on a hot summer day, the sort of ocean she just wanted to leap into and turn somersaults in until she laughed for joy. Lily hastily pulled off her heavy winter sweater, boots, and fireproof cape and jumped to her feet. She took another deep breath and then, for no reason at all, she burst out laughing and jumped up and down on the spot.

"Eydelen!" she shouted. "I'm in Eydelen, the

Valley of the Dragons!" Her voice echoed off the surrounding cliffs, and she ran madly around in a circle, dancing and clapping her hands. A warm breeze was blowing toward her, and she suddenly smelled a waft of perfume coming from a nearby belt of trees. Lily ran toward it. Sure enough, the smell was what she had thought it was: a scent and sight she had never thought to see again.

"Moon roses!" The moon rose trees were taller here than the ones in the orchards and gardens of Skellig Lir, and the gnarled ancient trees were growing wild. Lily ran through the forest in delight. She grabbed branches of trees and swung on them, she splashed in the streams and waded through hollows of delicate ferns until her senses were almost overloaded with the scent and the sight of the glorious pink-and-white blossom. It rained down over her face and covered the ground like confetti. This thought of weddings brought Lily up suddenly short. She was, after all, here for Queen Dragon's sake, not her own. Where was she, then? The thought had no sooner crossed Lily's mind than she heard the sound of familiar singing. She started hurrying through the trees toward it, and a minute or two later emerged to the sound of running water on yet another jutting-out piece of cliff top.

Queen Dragon was sitting on a flat rock at the bottom, swaying back and forth under a water-fall with her wings extended and her eyes closed. Whatever her other talents, Queen Dragon had never been much of a singer, but Lily lay down on the cliff top and waited until she reached the end of her song. Queen Dragon stepped out from under the waterfall. She looked up, saw Lily watching her, and blushed even redder than her scales.

"Lily! I didn't realize you were awake."

"Don't worry." Lily sat up and swung her legs around so that they dangled over the cliff. "Queen Dragon, isn't this the most beautiful place you've ever seen? It's just like the Singing Wood, only better!"

Queen Dragon nodded. "I think we must be in Eydelen. Oh Lily, to think I almost didn't believe you—and now we're here! Look." She waved a claw at the cliff behind the waterfall. Lily gasped. It was shot through with fat streaks of pure gold. Queen Dragon spread her wings ecstatically above her head. "Cliffs, caves, and clear skies—and I can just smell the metal in these rocks; you just break them open and suck it out. All we need to do now is find King Dragon and my happiness will be complete!"

"He must be here somewhere." Lily looked up at the sky. A green winged shape was wheeling down over a cliff top on the opposite side of the valley, and a pulse of excitement started up in her throat at the sight. It was another dragon, the first sign that they were truly where they were meant to be. Queen Dragon, too, stared up at the flying shape. A look of intense hunger crossed over her scaly face, like that of a marooned sailor sighting a sail from his desert island.

"Annacondia," she said in a voice full of wonder. "Has to be. No one else was ever quite that color. She was one . . . She was one of King Dragon's companions."

"Then what are we waiting for?" Lily demanded. "Let's go and find her, straightaway!"

After General Sark had been marched away and lodged in a cell beneath Ashby Castle, King Lionel and Queen Evangeline continued their emergency meeting. Some tea and biscuits had been brought for them, but neither of them felt much like their usual after-dinner snack. The king was so distracted he drank an entire cup of tea without putting any sugar in it. Evangeline dabbled her currant biscuit in her own cup, then left it, uneaten, on her saucer.

"I'm afraid Sark's got us, Evie," said Lionel. "Funny. I never thought of him as being especially clever, but what he's done is absolutely brilliant. By bringing the Black Seal with him, he's got us trapped. If we don't help him, we're going to be invaded almost immediately. It's that simple."

"Then we must throw Sark out of Ashby," said Evangeline. "Get rid of him. Send him beyond our borders to somewhere where he can be someone else's problem."

"Whose?" said Lionel. "Who'd take him? It's no use, Evie. By now, Gordon will know Sark is here. We either have to stand and fight him—or go along with Sark's demands and give him what he wants."

"Go along with Sark?' said Evangeline in a panic. "How can we? Ashby can't invade the Black Empire. Gordon will have tanks, dragonets, and as many Black Squads as he needs. We don't even have a proper army—goodness, we don't even have Lily and Queen Dragon!"

"True. But Sark doesn't know that, and neither does Gordon," said the king. "Don't worry, Evie. I'm not going to let Sark blackmail us. But we may be able to stall him while we try and negotiate."

A light tap sounded on the door as he spoke. "Enter!" called the king, and the door of the council chamber was opened by a tall man with a friendly face. The king and queen immediately jumped to their feet.

"Trevor! How glad we are to see you! We've been thinking of you and Angela ever since we got your pigeon!"

"You won't be glad to see me when you've heard what I have to tell you," said Mr. Hartley ruefully. "I've been sent by Gordon with personal instructions to deliver this letter." He brought a creamy piece of parchment out of his pocket. It was sealed with a round black lump of sealing wax, crudely stamped with what looked like the portrait side of a coin.

"A declaration of war?" Lionel broke the seal

and read the letter. "Not quite. I must return the Black Seal and General Sark immediately or the armies of the Black Count will march upon Ashby within the week. I'm to send you back with my handwritten reply. Well. That's not much of a surprise. Oh dear. He points out that Angela is still in the Black Citadel. I hope she's all right."

"That's just bluster," said Mr. Hartley. "Angela was Gordon's foster mother. She's not a hostage, and whatever he says, Gordon is far too fond of her to ever hurt her. I left Angela helping the miners with their wounded. It was a bit of a shock for her to meet up with Gordon this time. You see, he is now grown-up."

"Grown up!" exclaimed Evangeline. "How can he be? Gordon's not much older than Lily!"

"He was the last time we saw him," said Mr. Hartley. "But not now. Don't forget, Gordon's been hiding in the past and more time has obviously gone by back then than it has in the present. I'd say he must be about twenty years old now. Certainly old enough to know what he's doing. He's an extremely determined young man."

"Good grief." Lionel looked shaken. "I had no idea of this. Has he joined forces with Manuelo?"

"Manuelo is certainly supporting him," said Mr. Hartley. "I'm not sure exactly why, though, and I'm still not sure who Manuelo is. It's a very closely guarded secret. I did wonder if it might be Veronica. She's Gordon's second in command, and she and Gordon are absolutely inseparable. But then I saw Veronica and Manuelo talking together, so I'm not sure now who Manuelo is."

"Don't worry," said the king. "I've got a feeling we'll find out soon enough."

Lily and Queen Dragon flew over Eydelen toward the cliff where they had seen the other dragon. The valley itself was enormous. It stretched as far as Lily could see, a great rift in the earth that shimmered blue and green in the morning sunshine. Every cliff top was covered with trees and woods, and the valley sides were riddled with caves, clefts, and caverns. Huge waterfalls poured over the cliff edges, and a broad, beautiful river ran along the valley floor, so clear that Queen Dragon could almost see the fish that swam there.

"Over there, Queen Dragon." Lily pointed. "She flew out from behind that bit of rock."

Queen Dragon banked and steered toward the outcropping. Sure enough, a huge opening could be seen in the cliff face just behind it. Queen Dragon glided down and landed neatly on the doorstep. She shook her wings and folded them up, then dropped her head so Lily could alight.

"I don't think anyone's home." Lily's voice echoed softly around an enormous chamber with a high domed roof. Soft, silvery sand shifted under her feet as she walked forward into the cavern, and a hole overhead, fringed with plants, let in light and air. There was no dragon. But in the middle of the chamber was something else, round and translucent as a pearl. It was a dragon's egg. Warm sand had been carefully piled around it and it shimmered in the light that shone down from the hole in the roof above like a pale jewel in a princess's coronet. Lily stood and looked at it in awe.

"An egg." Queen Dragon's eyes were full of tears. "Oh, Lily, it must be centuries since I've seen one. This is the most wonderful moment yet."

Lily knelt in the sand beside her. Something was moving beneath the soft membrane, the baby dragon that was about to be born. They were both so captivated by the sight that it took a moment for them to realize that they were not alone. Then Lily heard something scrape behind her and felt the temperature in the enclosed space shoot up. She turned and saw that another dragon had appeared in the entrance behind them.

It was the first healthy dragon Lily had seen since she had met Queen Dragon at the grommet factory. Like Queen Dragon then, this dragon was in the prime of her life and health, but where her encounter with Queen Dragon had left Lily rigid with fear, her first sight of this dragon left her speechless with wonder. Lily thought she was the most delicate, beautiful creature she had ever seen. Her scales were elusive shades of green and bronze, like the underside of a fern in dappled sunlight; her eyes were round and golden; and everything about her, from the dainty claws to the elegant barb on her tail, literally glowed with joy and peace. Lily felt a pang. In the presence of so much beauty, it was hard not to realize that, by dragon standards, Queen Dragon must be thought of as very plain.

For a long moment the newcomer looked at

Queen Dragon and Queen Dragon looked at her. At last the other dragon broke the silence. "Sinhault!" she breathed. "Sinhault Fierdaze! After all this time. You're here!"

"Annacondia!" Queen Dragon stumbled toward her, so swiftly that the sand flew up and scattered under her feet and tail. The two dragons almost collided. Their necks twined, and their wings beat at their sides. Boiling hot tears ran down both of their scaly faces and dropped into the sand. Lily hastily backed away before she got splashed.

"But how did you come here after all this time?" asked Annacondia, when she had recovered enough to speak. "Sinhault, dearest, it must have been thousands of years! How did you even know we were here?"

"Lily brought me. I couldn't have done it without her," Queen Dragon explained. "She had a vision of King Dragon. He told her that you were living here and that I was to come and join you."

"King Dragon?" A look of dismay came suddenly over Annacondia's face and for a moment Lily could have sworn there was fear in her liquid eyes. "You've come here to find King Dragon?"

"Yes. Don't you remember we were engaged? I've never forgotten him, Annacondia. Even though I didn't know whether he was alive or dead, for thousands of years I've thought of no one else. Of course I've come here to find King Dragon. He is the only reason I'm still alive."

"Sinhault, stop! Stop at once!" Annacondia burst out. "Oh, my dear, this is too terrible! I feel sick, sick, sick! I don't know how I can begin to tell you!"

Queen Dragon's crimson scales went ashen bronze. "Annacondia. Tell me the worst. Is King Dragon all right? Is he hurt, sick, injured? He's not—he's not *dead*, is he?"

"No, no! He's well; he's quite all right." Annacondia's voice shook as she said the words. "But there's something you need to know, and I don't know how to say it. You see, Sinhault, all of us here thought that you were dead. Including King Dragon. None of us expected to see you ever again."

"But I'm not dead, am I?" Queen Dragon sounded confused. "King Dragon will be pleased to see me, won't he?'

"Oh, Sinhault, I'm sure he will be more pleased

about this than anything he has heard in a thousand years." Annacondia reached out with a gentle wingtip. "But things have changed here since we've seen you. Our lives in Eydelen are different beyond anything you could even begin to imagine, and King Dragon's life and mine have changed most of all. You see, this is not just my egg, Sinhault. It's King Dragon's, too. King Dragon is my husband."

chapter five

The Vale of Eydelen

"Your husband?" Queen Dragon repeated Annacondia's last words in a stricken voice. She sounded to Lily as if she did not quite believe them. "I don't understand. How can he be your husband? King Dragon is engaged to me!"

"He *was* engaged to you, dearest," said Annacondia gently. "But he thought he'd lost you. When we left the Great War of the Dragons, it seemed as though nobody was going to survive. You cannot blame King Dragon if he thought you were dead."

"But I did survive!" Queen Dragon cried. "So

did Serpentine Bridgestock and a heap of others. I never gave up on King Dragon. Are you really telling me that he gave up on me?"

Annacondia sighed. "No, Sinhault. But I am telling you he and I have been married for nearly two hundred and fifty years, and that our first egg is lying there in that nest. I am sorry. I feel terrible. But there is nothing I can do."

Queen Dragon blinked and shook her head. "No. I suppose there isn't." She started blundering toward the entrance. "Excuse me, Annacondia. I have to think about this. I have—" She launched herself distractedly off the ledge and flew away. Annacondia and Lily stood watching her go.

"Poor Sinhault!" Annacondia's scaly cheeks were wet with tears. "How terrible this must be for her. She must be feeling devastated."

"Her heart will be broken." Lily felt devastated, too. All the morning's happiness had vanished, and she wished she had never come. Above all, she felt bewildered. She had been so convinced they were doing the right thing, yet their coming to Eydelen had ended in disaster. Nothing was working out as she had expected. Lily could not understand how she had been so completely wrong.

She turned to Annacondia and asked the only question she could think of. "King Dragon. Will he speak to me? I think he needs to be told what is going on."

As soon as Annacondia had turned her egg in the warm sand, she and Lily took off from the cliff-top aerie. They spiraled down for several hundred feet, then flew along the valley, tracking the crystal river that flowed along it. As they passed a secluded cleft in the rocks, Lily glimpsed two other dragons frolicking in the water. They were the same crimson color as Queen Dragon, but not as big.

"That's Sandfire and his sister, Snaketooth," said Annacondia, when Lily pointed them out to her. "Their parents are Scaletooth and Petrified Snaketongue, who came with us into the valley. They're twins, born out of a single egg. That's most unusual for dragons. It only happens every thousand years or so."

"How many of you are there altogether?" Lily asked her.

"Only five of us came into the valley after the battle," Annacondia replied. "But we've been joined by a couple of other dragons who found their way here, like Queen Dragon did this morning. And of course, some of us have had children. There are about fifteen of us, now. We live separately, scattered along the valley, though we all see each other regularly. This is where King Dragon and I live, here."

She veered away from the valley into a tree-fringed cavern at the foot of the cliff. Like the aerie, it was large and light with a neatly sanded floor and piles of metal sorted in niches along the walls. Everything was incredibly neat, quite unlike Queen Dragon's own cavern under the volcano, where centuries of treasure were jumbled every which way in an enormous heap. A musical humming could be heard at the back of the cave. As Lily and Annacondia entered, it broke off and someone started moving toward them.

"Annacondia," said a rich, gentle rumble of a voice. "I had not expected you back so soon."

King Dragon emerged from the back of the cave. Lily's knees went weak. Her past dreams and visions were nothing compared to her first sight of King Dragon in the flesh. His burnished scales glowed, and his eyes were so wise and golden that Lily felt as if she were going to drown in them. Everything about him was perfectly proportioned, from his sleek muscled body to the top of his golden head. Lily could no longer wonder that Queen Dragon had loved him for over two thousand years. She was already almost half in love with him herself.

"A human!" said King Dragon in a wondering voice. "A human girl. Why, Annacondia, I have not seen such a thing in thousands of years! How could she come into Eydelen?"

"I do not know precisely," said Annacondia. "My dearest, I do not know how to tell you this, but she did not come alone. This is Lily Quench. She arrived here this morning with—with Sinhault Fierdaze!" Suddenly the emotion of the moment overcame her, and she burst into hysterical tears.

It was more than Lily could stand. She turned and ran out of the cave, the sound of Annacondia's weeping following her all the way down to the river. All she wanted was to find Queen Dragon and get away from Eydelen as quickly as she could, but there seemed little chance of her being able to do either of these things. Lily ran into the long grass by the river. By now she was crying, too, and she flung herself down and buried her face in her arms. She was still weeping half an hour later when she heard the grass rustle behind her. Lily sat up and saw King Dragon regarding her sympathetically with his golden eyes.

"Annacondia has told me everything, Lily," he said. "She's gone back to the aerie in case Sinhault returns. And I have sent some of the younger dragons off to search the valley for her. I'm sorry everyone is so upset, Lily, but I promise you I will do everything I can to make things better."

Lily looked up at him through her tears. "I don't understand," she said brokenly. "I saw you in my vision. I spoke to you. You told us to come here. Why did you say that if you didn't mean for us to come?"

"Ah." A look of comprehension flitted across King Dragon's face. "Annacondia mentioned something about this. Lily, it may be hard for you to understand this, but seeing a vision is not the same as talking to the real me. Your vision was merely meant for guidance and encouragement;

it is not in my power to ask for Sinhault to come. But this I do know: it has always been said that no one comes to Eydelen unless they are meant to find a way here. If that is true, then there is a purpose to your being here, a reason for you both to have come."

"I suppose so," said Lily. "But it's hard to see a reason at the moment."

"The Vale of Eydelen *is* the home of the dragons," King Dragon pointed out. "However upset Sinhault may be now, it must be better for her to be here among other dragons than to live in the outside world. Eydelen is one of the great and secret places, the most beautiful and magical of them all. Surely you realize what a special place this is?"

"Yes," admitted Lily. "I do. And I know that it's right for Queen Dragon to stay here. The only problem is, you might have some trouble persuading her."

"I will speak to her about it," King Dragon said. He looked up. Two young dragons, one green and one black, were spiraling down out of the sky toward them. Lily could not help noticing that one of them, the green dragon, was flying awkwardly, as if her wing had been somehow injured. They landed on the rock not far away from them, and the black dragon hurried toward King Dragon.

"Wormwood," King Dragon greeted him. "Have you had any success in your search?"

The young dragon shook his head. Then his eye fell on Lily, half hidden behind King Dragon's bulk, and he recoiled, trembling.

"Another one!" he cried. "Another human!" He started back, and Lily stopped in her tracks. Though she had done nothing to deserve it, Wormwood was actually afraid of her.

"Others? What others?" Lily asked. As she spoke, the green dragon, Snaketail, stumbled forward, trailing her injured wing upon the ground. Her yellow eyes were wild with pain and terror.

"Fire," she croaked. "They hit me with fire. Look." She lifted her wing, and Lily gasped. Its membrane was peppered with neat round holes of a kind that Lily, in her wildest dreams, had never expected to see again.

They were the same as the ones she had seen on Queen Dragon's wing at the magicians' pyramids. Wormwood and Snaketail had been attacked by magic.

King Lionel of Ashby had had a bad night's sleep.

He and Evangeline had gone to bed at midnight after feeding Elizabeth. Both of them were tired, but neither felt much like sleeping. They had kept each other awake, and though the queen had eventually nodded off, the king had tossed and turned under the coverlets for hours. Now Lionel sat in front of the window in his private sitting room, watching the sun come up over the castle battlements. On the desk in front of him lay a piece of paper embossed with the royal motto, *BY QUENCHING WE RULE*. Lionel had taken the cap off his fountain pen several times, but so far he had failed to write more than the date and half a dozen words.

In his heart of hearts, he had always known it would come to this. Ashby was such a tiny country, so insignificant in the larger scheme of things, that it had been a mad dream to think it could keep its independence long. Lionel had thought he was the man for the job, but the longer he was king, the harder he realized his task really was. He did not believe he had been wrong to try to stand up for what he believed in, but it troubled him deeply that so many other people stood to fall with him when he failed. Above all, he feared for Evangeline and the tiny princess, asleep and dreaming milky dreams in her cradle. When he thought of what might happen to her, Lionel quailed so that he almost gave up.

At length he took the lid off his pen again, sucked the end thoughtfully, and began to write. The king worked on for half an hour or so, crossing out words and crumpling several sheets of paper until at last he had what he wanted. Then he went to the cupboard where he kept his royal seal and sealing wax. The melting wax hissed and spat as he dropped it onto the parchment, and the stick caught fire and had to be blown out. Lionel stamped the wax and returned his seal to its box. He added another object from his pocket, then closed the lid and locked it safely away.

By now the sun was well above the battlements, and the castle was starting to stir. Lionel pushed a button on his desk. It rang twice, and, after a few minutes, there was a tap on the door.

"Give this letter to Mr. Hartley," said the king

to Jason the chamberlain. "He'll know what to do with it. And call a meeting of the Royal Council. It's time to mobilize the troops."

chapter six

Old Enemies

Gordon, the Black Count, stood at his tower window looking down on the citadel courtyard. A burned-out tank was sitting in the middle of its broken-up concrete, there was barbed wire in heaps, and bonfires burned at several points. Blue-clad miners and Black Squad soldiers were working together in gangs, raking up rubble and shoring up wobbly walls to keep them from falling down. Five days after Sark's surrender, they were still no closer to cleaning up the mess, especially as it had been snowing heavily for much of the time.

Gordon closed his window, cutting off the icy blast of winter air. He went over to the fire and stirred it with a poker, looked at the pile of paperwork on the table, and wearily ran his hands through his short dark hair. Everything here was the same as it had been when he had left nine months before—and yet, it was all incredibly different. In the past, where he had been living, nine long years had gone by. Gordon was now grown up, and it seemed unreal to be back in the same old room where he had done his lessons, dreamed his lonely dreams, and fantasized about how he was going to please his father. Gordon's father had once meant more to him than anyone else in the world. It was hard for him to adjust to the fact that, in this time, the people he was speaking to on a daily basis had clear and sometimes extremely unpleasant memories of him. Of late, Gordon had been upset to realize how hard it was to remember exactly what his father looked like. He was not a sentimental person, but almost his first action on reclaiming the citadel had been to find a photo and put it in his uniform pocket.

Gordon took the photo out now and looked

at it. It was a nice shot, taken on his eleventh birthday only a few days before his father had died. They were standing beside a shiny new motorbike, and the young Gordon was holding a helmet and looking very pleased with himself. His father wasn't smiling—he had never smiled, that was his way—but he looked relaxed and had his arm protectively around Gordon's shoulder. Now that he was grown up, Gordon couldn't help wondering whether his father had in fact been *too* protective. He had certainly spoiled his only son. When he had first gone into his old rooms, Gordon had been shocked to see how many toys he had owned. It was horrible to realize what a spoiled brat he had been.

"I can't believe you put up with me," he had blurted out to Angela Hartley, his old foster mother, who had been there when the rooms were opened up.

"It wasn't always easy," Angela admitted in her honest way, and though she had given him a friendly hug, Gordon had been mortified. He had ordered all the toys to be sent to the mining encampments, and later he had gone out riding on a motorbike similar to the one his father had given him. The cold and the wind and the speed had made him somehow feel better, but Veronica had been furious. Back in the past, when they had served together in Count Raymond Longshank's army, she had been a cavalry officer. She did not trust cars or tanks or newfangled forms of transport, and, like so many other things in this time, the motorbike had frightened her because she did not understand it.

Someone knocked at the door. Gordon looked up from the window and saw Veronica herself standing in the doorway. She was dressed in thick gray tights with a miniskirt, sweater, and red boots, and her dark hair was braided down her back. Gordon, who was used to seeing her in uniform, thought she looked very nice. He smiled at her, and Veronica briefly smiled back at him. Then her face went serious again, and she shut the door carefully and locked it.

"Did you find the Black Seal?" asked Gordon.

"No." Veronica sat down by the fire. Gordon joined her, and they stuck out their feet companionably to the blaze. "I've had my most trusted miners search the citadel from top to bottom, and there is no sign of it anywhere. It could have been destroyed—but I have to say, I think that's unlikely."

"I agree," said Gordon. "Sark definitely took it with him; there's no doubt about it. Here, Ronnie. This is from Lionel of Ashby. Read it." He handed her an envelope with a broken seal. Gordon had taught Veronica to read while they had been on campaign back in the past with Count Raymond's army. She was not very good at it, but since most people in her time could not read at all, she was very proud of the accomplishment. Gordon knew this, and because he loved her and because all the things that had gone wrong for him had finally taught him patience, he waited while she slowly read it through.

Dear Gordon, [Lionel had written]

As requested, I am sending this letter with Trevor Hartley. I confirm that General Sark is here in Ashby Water and that he is currently my prisoner. Unfortunately, I cannot return him to you at this time.

I am sorry you feel the need to threaten Ashby and would like to think we can sort things out without further fighting. You may send your suggestions back to me with Mr. Hartley or by pigeon, as convenient.

Looking forward to your earliest reply,
I remain,
Yours sincerely,
Lionel R.

Veronica wrinkled her brow. "He doesn't mention the Black Seal."

"No. But he's got it, all the same," said Gordon. "Sark is Lionel's enemy as much as ours, Ronnie. The king should have sent him straight back to me the moment he received my letter. The fact that he didn't means that Sark is giving him something in return. But whether the seal is in Lionel's keeping or Sark's, it makes no difference. The Black Seal *is* in Ashby Water. And if I'm going to get it back, we need to go there."

"All right." Veronica sighed. Her face was drawn, and Gordon thought she looked very tired. Impulsively he took her hand and squeezed it.

"You've been so good to me, Ronnie," he said. "Putting up with that pig, Raymond, leaving your own time, fighting all those wars. When I am truly Black Count, I shall make it up to you, I promise."

"You don't have to make it up to me." Veronica rested her forehead briefly on his shoulder. "But I'll be glad if Ashby Water is the last battle. I'm so tired of fighting. And Murdo, my brother—now we're both in this time, he's being terribly difficult. He's following me everywhere. He doesn't understand why I'm suddenly grown up. And I think he suspects about Manuelo." Her eyes followed Gordon's to a black, hooded cape that was hanging on the back of a chair, and they were both silent for a moment.

"With luck we won't need Manuelo for very much longer," said Gordon quietly. "Will you come with me to Ashby, Ronnie? Will you fight with me one last time?"

"You know I will, even if it isn't the last time," said Veronica. "I love you, Gordon. And nobody is going to get in the way of our plans."

A light covering of cloud had come up over Eydelen in the hours since Lily's arrival. It cast shadows over the valley where Snaketail and

Wormwood had encountered the intruders and gave Lily, King Dragon, and Wormwood somewhere to hide as they flew toward it. Lily held on tightly as she and King Dragon dived through the moist canopy. King Dragon was much faster than Queen Dragon, and his flight was smoother, more powerful, and more nearly silent.

Ahead of them, Wormwood alighted behind a spur of rock. King Dragon and Lily landed beside him. At the foot of the cliff below was a shady hollow. There was too much rock there for the moon rose trees to put down roots, and it was filled with silvery bushes, tall ferns, and a few saplings. A plume of smoke rose up from between the fronds. Lily could not see what was causing it, but there was obviously someone there.

"We saw the humans camping here earlier this morning," whispered Wormwood. "There were two of them. We flew down to have a look, and one of them started throwing fireballs at us."

King Dragon's face was grim. "What else?"

Wormwood shook his head. "Nothing. We flew away at once. I've never seen humans before. These ones were very ugly."

"They must have come here after you and

Queen Dragon, Lily," said King Dragon. "No human has visited Eydelen since our arrival. I cannot believe that these enemies—old enemies, if I am not mistaken—should arrive on the same day as you, by coincidence."

Unhappily, Lily agreed. "I think I know who one of them might be. Wait here." She climbed carefully down the cliff. It was not too steep or difficult, and about halfway down she found a place where she could crouch behind some rocks and look directly into the campsite. Lily saw a woman sitting by a fire, stirring something in a tiny pot that was nestled among the flames. As she watched, a shadow passed over the ground below her, and she saw a man glide in on wings that looked like a dragon's.

Lily's stomach churned. She had recognized the woman immediately: the witch, Aunt Cassy, whom she had last met in the past at Mote Ely Castle. The man she would not have recognized at all but for the beautiful green wings that he was wearing. When Lily had last seen Roger the magician, only a couple of months before, he had been young and fresh-faced. Now he looked ancient, with tufts of graying hair and horrible scars on his wrinkled skin. Roger was the enemy who had nearly killed Queen Dragon in an aerial battle after the destruction of the Magicians' Pyramid. Now it looked as if he had almost done the same to Wormwood and Snaketail.

Quickly and silently, Lily climbed back up the cliff to her dragon companions.

"Wings!" exclaimed Wormwood, when she reported what she had seen. "Where would a human get wings from?"

"It's a long story," said Lily. She and King Dragon exchanged glances. He looked grimmer than ever, and she thought he might have guessed whose wings Roger was using. Baba, the pitiful imprisoned dragon she and Queen Dragon had met at the Magicians' Pyramid, had been Annacondia's sister. "I don't think I could bear to tell you. You have to act quickly, King Dragon. Roger is one of the magicians who built the Eye Stones, the people who put the Golden Child at Dragon's Downfall and caused the Great War of the Dragons. And Aunt Cassy is no friend to dragons either. They're evil people. You have to flame them now, before it's too late."

"Act, yes," said King Dragon. "But flame them?

No, Lily. A thousand times no! We must find another way of forcing them out of our valley."

Lily stared at him in disbelief. "King Dragon, don't you understand? It was Roger and his friends who started the Great War of the Dragons. Aunt Cassy tried to kill Queen Dragon so she could steal her blood. You cannot let them stay here in Eydelen! If you don't flame them, they will kill you all, or worse!"

"I cannot and I will not," said King Dragon. "Listen to me, Lily. We here in Eydelen are the last of our kind. Perhaps there are a few others like Queen Dragon, hiding in miserable lairs in the outside world, but they are the exception now, and the future of the dragons lies here. You have heard of the Great War of the Dragons. Sinhault will have told you how my companions and I went through the Eye Stone in the heat of the battle, how we sought help, and how we were tricked by Roger and his fellow magicians when we asked them for assistance. We were betrayed by Annacondia's own sister, Baba, and we lost our companion, Balefire, to the treachery of the magicians, yet somehow, in the midst of all the slaughter and the despair, we held on to hope. Can you imagine, Lily, when we escaped and came to this place, what it felt like to us?

"On the day we found Eydelen, we took an oath. We swore, all five of us, that we would never again kill or harm another living thing, that we would never fight among ourselves, and that our children would be brought up to do the same. And we promised that if any one of us who had taken the oath ever broke it, then all the dragons would leave Eydelen and never come back."

Lily looked up at him in dismay. King Dragon's face was deadly serious, and she realized he meant every word he said. But somehow, despite everything, she could not stop opening her mouth to protest once more. King Dragon cut her off before she could say a word.

"We took that oath in earnest, Lily. Living or dying, we mean to keep it. The magicians may be evil, but they must be allowed to live. Leave them now and come with me. We must return to my cave and wait for Queen Dragon to be found."

Under the silvery canopy of ferns, as far away from the forest of moon rose trees as they could manage to get, the magicians Roger and Cassy were sitting by a small campfire. It was made of green wood, so it should not have been burning at all, but the flames were a weird purple color that both Queen Dragon and Lily would immediately have recognized as magical. Cassy was cooking something dark and liquid in a small saucepan. It smelled horrible. Roger, who had stripped off his wings and pushed them back into their folds for storage, was sitting glumly watching her from a clump of rock.

"It's not going to work."

"It'll work," said Cassy shortly. She stirred the potion with a stick. "It may not be as effective as Joscelin's longevity potion, but it's always worked for me."

"Yes, and look at you. You're as ugly as sin."

Cassy's wrinkled face flushed red. "You're no oil painting yourself these days," she snapped. "Where have your good looks gone, Mr. Handsome? Primping and preening in front of your mirror like a girl. You think we didn't see you? Back in the old days, Morgan and I used to laugh at you until we nearly wet ourselves."

"At least I had good looks once," said Roger. "Unlike some people. Anyway, it's your own fault you look the way you do. If you hadn't been greedy, you'd have had the proper longevity potion like the rest of us. Joscelin would never have thrown you out if you hadn't killed Morgan in those tunnels under the lighthouse."

"Morgan was a thief," said Cassy coldly. "She stole that magic book we took from the Library of Skellig Lir. I went after her to bring it back, and she attacked me."

Roger's lip curled. "Come on, Cassy. Don't pretend. You were the one who stole the book. Morgan was chasing you, and you stuck your knife into her. You were always greedy and vicious and bordering on mad. It doesn't look like much has changed, does it?"

Cassy stopped stirring and rounded on him. "If I'm mad," she hissed, "then why did you keep in touch with me? Why did you steal the blood from Baba, your tame dragon, so that I could drink it and stay alive?" Roger was silent, and she jabbed him viciously in the chest with her bony finger. "It's because you helped kill Morgan," she hissed, "and I could have told Joscelin at any moment. Where would you have been then, handsome?"

"In the same hole as you," said Roger. "Literally. From where I'm sitting now, it would almost be worth it."

"Just so we know where we stand," said Cassy. She took the tiny cauldron off the fire and ladled its steaming contents into two small cups. "There. That's the last of the dragon's blood you rescued from the pyramids. Drink your medicine down; that's a good boy."

Roger made a face. He took the cup in one hand and, holding his nose with the other, swallowed the dragon's blood down in one choking gulp. Cassy swilled hers around in the cup like a vintage wine, then casually tossed it down. Roger shuddered.

"I don't know how you can do that."

"You'd better get used to it if you want to stay alive," said Cassy bluntly. "We need more dragon's blood, and we need it soon. We didn't find Lily Quench's dragon on that island, but maybe we'll find her here. If not, one of those other dragons will do. We must catch a dragon quickly, Roger. If we don't, we die."

chapter seven

The Egg

"Is this the worst day of my life?" Queen Dragon asked herself. She sat huddled in a dusty cave in the cliff face, staring at the light that filtered down past the entrance. The ground was wet with her tears, and she could not have summoned a flame to save her life. "I'm inclined to think it is. Of course, there have been other bad days, lots of them. You can't live for three thousand years and not have things go wrong. Losing my friend, Serpentine Bridgestock, was awful. The Great War of the Dragons was even worse. That was the day I lost King Dragon the first time, the day things changed for dragons forever. And meeting Baba at the Magicians' Pyramid, and being turned into a mosaic with Lily—that was pretty horrible, too. We've been through some scary times together, Lily and I. But really, on the face of it, I don't think anything compares with this morning. This is, absolutely, definitely, positively, without a doubt the worst day of my entire life."

Queen Dragon spoke these last words aloud and burst into tears again. Hot salty water ran down her cheeks and dripped, steaming, onto the cave floor, her shoulders heaved, and her wings twitched involuntarily at her sides. But no one came to comfort her. Even Lily didn't know where she was, and Queen Dragon wanted it to stay that way. If it had not been for Lily, she would never have come here, would never have had to go through this terrible heartache. Queen Dragon was too kind-spirited to bear a grudge. She knew that Lily had tried to act for the best and that she had made enormous sacrifices to come here. But Lily, for all her understanding of dragons, was still a human. She would never understand what it meant to feel the weight of every one of her three thousand years pressing down on her, crushing and grinding her dearest hopes into oblivion. *No human could love like a dragon*, thought Queen Dragon dully. Their life spans simply didn't afford them the scope.

Something thumped and scraped at the cave entrance, and the light went dim. A red dragon with a friendly face and a dumpy figure had landed among the rocks and ferns.

"Sinhault. Is that you?"

"Hello, Kniphofia," said Queen Dragon miserably. "Long time, no see."

"I was wondering if you were hiding around here somewhere. Hear you had a bit of an upset," said Kniphofia Scarlet. Queen Dragon nodded. Kniphofia sat down beside her and made a *tsk-tsk*-ing noise at the sight of her tearstained face. Queen Dragon started sobbing again. This time, however, it was with a sense of relief, for she had known Kniphofia since they were hatchlings. Nippy was sensible and kind, and she was a dragon. She would understand. Queen Dragon's head dropped onto Kniphofia's shoulder, and for the next five minutes or so she bawled unashamedly, choking out the story of her lonely exile, Lily's vision, and their arrival in Eydelen that morning.

"And the worst of it is, this place is so *beautiful*," Queen Dragon finished. "It seems—*sinful* somehow, to be here and feel so unhappy. But I can't help myself, Nippy. I've waited so long to find this place. And now that I'm here, everything I've dreamed of and hoped for seems to have gone wrong."

"You're right about Eydelen being beautiful," said Kniphofia. "It *is* special. It's like the Singing Wood, one of the few secret places that have scarcely changed since the beginning of the world. But it is still part of the world, Sinhault. It is easy to be happy here, but it is also possible to be sad. When we came here after the war, it took us centuries to settle down and feel at peace. You must give yourself time to get over this."

"But why did he do it, Nippy?" Queen Dragon wailed. "Why?"

It was a long moment before Kniphofia answered. "You know, Sinhault, when we came here, both Annacondia and I were still single. I'm not ashamed to say we were both in love with King Dragon. You know what he's like—how could anyone not love him? But for centuries, all he could think of was you. Just the thought of you, the mention of your name, used to make him cry, and he would fly away and hide in the canyons for days at a time. But broken hearts do heal, Sinhault. Even dragon hearts. Even mine. Well, I'm not stupid. Who'd pick me over Annacondia? It was hard at first, seeing them together, but I got used to it. And honestly, it's not so bad not being married. I enjoy my life. Poor Scaletooth's spent most of the last two thousand years hatching eggs. You can imagine how boring that is."

"I suppose so," said Queen Dragon in a small voice. "But I still don't think I can live here. Nippy, have you seen my friend Lily Quench? I left her in Annacondia's aerie. I shouldn't have run off the way I did. She'll be worried about me."

"The small human? I believe she's with King Dragon," said Kniphofia. "Come and I'll take you to them."

Queen Dragon set up a wail of protest. "Nippy, I can't. I can't see him—"

"You can't hide here forever, Sinhault—" Kniphofia began, but she never finished her sentence. A harsh cry sounded somewhere along the valley. It was a high and dreadful note borne of desperation and terror, a call to help that overruled every other feeling, a cry that could not be ignored. Queen Dragon's eyes locked with Kniphofia's, and her own distress evaporated.

"It's the Dragons' Cry of Summoning," she whispered. "It's Annacondia."

From their throne room windows, King Lionel and Queen Evangeline stood watching the swelling crowd in the castle bailey. Old men and women, children, babies and their parents had been gathering there since first thing in the morning. The adults carried tents and backpacks, the children school bags crammed with food and warm clothes, dolls and teddy bears. By royal decree, the people of Ashby Water were leaving the town. War was coming, and none of those who stood in the throne room with the king and queen were silly enough to think that they were going to be able to stop it.

King Lionel turned from the window and looked at his councillors. Mr. Hartley had returned from the Black Mountains that morning in a dragonet, bringing with him Gordon's formal declaration of war. With him was Sir Jason Pearl, the chamberlain, and General Sir Wilibald Zouche, newly admitted to the council and in charge of Ashby's army. The only two who were missing were Lily and Queen Dragon.

"When all the evacuees are gathered, Jason, I want you to leave immediately," said the king. "I want everyone out of Ashby Water by nightfall. They shouldn't need to take much with them. The caves in the Ashby Hills are already provisioned."

"Lucky our winters are so mild," said Evangeline. "I don't imagine a night in the open's going to be much fun for all those grannies with their rheumaticky joints."

"Better a few cold noses and aching bones than being here when Gordon's army arrives," said Lionel. "The only people we can afford to have in Ashby Water right now are the ones who can fight." He addressed the councillors, who were waiting for his orders. "Sir Wilibald, distribute the Quenching Drops, and see if the patrols have finished sealing off the roads into town. Mr. Hartley, you check what's happening with the sandbagging. I want all public buildings secured by morning. Sir Jason, send out a general order for all households to take in extra water. In the last siege, the Black Squads cut off the water supply. People had nothing to drink but the sludge from the canal."

"Right away, Your Majesty." One by one, the councillors bowed and filed out of the room. The king took a pencil and notebook from his pocket. He crossed a couple of items off a very long list and added several more to the bottom. He did not say anything, but Evangeline was close enough to see how shaky his writing was and how his hand trembled as he put the notebook away. The baby princess burped in her sling and opened her eyes to a tiny slit. Evangeline stroked Elizabeth's downy head, and the princess gave a little gurgling sigh and fell asleep again.

Lionel turned back to the window. He stood grasping the sill, his forehead against the pane. Jason was down in the courtyard now, shouting at the evacuees through a megaphone. Evangeline looked at her husband's somber expression, reflected in the glass. She held the baby gently against her body and waited.

"I wish you'd go with them, Evie. Those hill

caves are the best refuge we've got. I'd feel so much better knowing that you and Elizabeth were safe."

"I can't," said Evangeline. "I'm the queen, Lionel. If I leave Ashby Water now, everyone will think that there's no hope. I know Gordon's army is bigger than ours. I know we don't know very much about fighting. All we really have are Lily's Quenching Drops, and there aren't even enough of those to really make a difference. But I have to stay. You, of all people, should understand why."

Lionel sighed. He turned from the window and Evangeline saw that his eyes were red. He put his arm around her and hugged her. Then he stroked the little princess's cheek with his other finger.

"I know, Evie. But it's not just us anymore. We have to think about Elizabeth."

"I am thinking about her." Evangeline's voice shook. "I don't want to, but I know I must. I'll make plans. If Ashby Castle is besieged, Elizabeth won't be here. But I must be."

"I'll be glad to have you," said Lionel. "Because it's not 'if' now, Evie. It's 'when.'"

Queen Dragon and Kniphofia dived toward the aerie like a pair of crimson thunderbolts. The sound of Annacondia's Cry of Summoning still echoed through the valley, and Eydelen rang with the cries of dragons answering her call. The Cry of Summoning was more than a simple call for help. It could be made only in a dragon's hour of most desperate need, and any dragon hearing it had no choice but to come to the aid of the one in danger.

Queen Dragon counted the fourteen responses as they came. The last three were the farthest away, and with a faint heart she realized she recognized two of them. "King Dragon," panted Kniphofia. "That's Wormwood with him. I don't know who the third one is, though."

"It's Lily." Queen Dragon felt pride mingle with her concern. "I taught her how to make the cry—oh, ages ago. She even used it once, when she needed help. You were right. She must be with King Dragon."

"They're quite a long way off," Kniphofia said. "It sounds as if they're coming from his cave. We must have been the closest—*whoa!*" Something red hot and sizzling whizzed past Kniphofia's ear, and she swerved to one side. "What was that?"

"A fireball." The crimson color drained from

Queen Dragon's face. The memory of her midair battle with the magician, Roger, at the Magicians' Pyramid was fresh enough to make her heart beat with terror. She had been closer to death that day than at almost any other time in her entire three thousand years. But what was Roger—if it *was* Roger—doing here? Queen Dragon ducked into a bank of cloud and heard a sizzle as several fireballs followed her through the vapor. "Quick, Nippy. Follow me. If those fireballs hit your wings, they'll cut right through the membrane. You'll be grounded!"

"Help!" A dragon voice shouted above them, and two more dragons swooped down to join them. It was Sandfire and his sister Snaketooth, a toothsome young dragon richly speckled with gold. "We're being attacked!"

"Who by?" demanded Kniphofia. "Did you see them?"

Snaketooth's golden eyes were wet with tears. "It's two human magicians. A man with wings and a woman with long gray hair. I saw them in the rocks outside Annacondia's aerie. Kniphofia, how did they get here? What should we do?"

"Attack them, of course!" Queen Dragon

interrupted before Kniphofia could even open her mouth. "There's four of us and only two of them. If we loop back through the cloud and fly down, we can catch them by surprise and flame them."

"Flame them?" Snaketooth panicked. "We can't flame them! We'll kill them!"

"Of course we'll kill them!" exclaimed Queen Dragon angrily. "What sort of a pathetic excuse for a dragon are you, girl? Annacondia's in danger; she's just made the Cry of Summoning. It's up to us to save her! Besides, those magicians are the greatest enemies dragonkind has ever had! What do you mean, you can't flame them, you boob!"

"Don't you speak to my sister like that!" shouted Sandfire. "She's right. We can't attack them!"

"Can't? Or won't?"

"Sinhault, you don't understand," said Kniphofia. "Snaketooth is right. We can't flame the magicians. We've taken an oath of peace."

"Oath of peace, fiddlesticks!" Queen Dragon started ducking and swerving as they emerged from the cloud bank. Fiery missiles were flying thick and fast now, and she marked the spot among the rocks from which they were coming.

Beside her, there was a yelp as Snaketooth took a direct hit on her right flank. "You mean we're supposed to let them do this to us? Oh, for goodness' sake, I'll do it myself!"

Queen Dragon flipped lithely sideways and veered off in the opposite direction. As she had expected, Roger kept hurling his fire at the other dragons, flinging only the occasional bolt at her. She hurtled into another cloud bank, looped around, and emerged on the other side, directly above Annacondia's aerie. Hoarse, dreadful screams were coming from inside, and she heard the unmistakable sizzle of more fireballs inside the cave. Then for the first time she glimpsed Roger, crouched among the rocks at the opening. Queen Dragon pulled in her enormous wings and dived in for the kill.

"Creep!" she screamed at the top of her enormous lungs. *"Monster!"*

Roger saw her coming. He yelled with fright, jumped to his feet, and launched himself into the air. Queen Dragon knew from her previous encounter with him that he was a dangerous flyer, but he seemed less quick this time, and he made no attempt to attack her while he was flying. He looked different, older than at their last encounter, and his face was scarred and ugly. Queen Dragon felt a spurt of satisfaction as she realized their battle at the pyramids had left its mark on him. She drew a deep breath in through her nostrils, opened her mouth, and flamed.

"No! Sinhault, no! *Don't do it!*" The other dragons were screaming at her, imploring her to stop as they alighted on the rocks surrounding the aerie, but Queen Dragon kept breathing fire until there was no breath left in her. As the last sputtering flame shot between her teeth, she glimpsed movement in the corner of her eye. Aunt Cassy was emerging from the cave, jumping down the rocks like a ten-year-old. A curved knife was in her hand, the same knife she had tried to kill Queen Dragon with at Mote Ely Castle. The three other dragons sat watching in horror. Then Kniphofia gave a cry of alarm and darted into the aerie.

"Get her!" Queen Dragon screamed to Sandfire and Snaketongue. "You gutless wonders! Do I have to do *everything* myself?"

"You killed him!" Snaketongue was almost hysterical. "You killed him! You've cursed the valley! Murderer! *Murderer!*"

Queen Dragon landed beside her, and she flinched away. But there was no time to confront Snaketongue now. Queen Dragon looked down and saw something trickling out of the cave entrance. It was blood. Dragon's blood. Queen Dragon's heart seemed to turn over and fall in the sand at her feet.

"Annacondia!" She shoved the shivering Snaketongue aside and hastened into the cave. It was dark inside, and there was a dreadful noise coming from somewhere ahead. It took a moment for Queen Dragon to realize it was Kniphofia. She was sprawled on the floor just inside the entrance, and she was weeping and shrieking by turns. A horrible, sick feeling washed over Queen Dragon, but though everything screamed at her to go back, some irresistible need impelled her forward. She smelled blood and death, and then she stepped in something hot, liquid, and sticky and knew what she was about to find.

Annacondia was lying in the middle of the

aerie, wings akimbo, in a sea of blood and fallen rock. She had been stabbed several times in her soft underbelly, and her wings had been slashed to pieces, but though these cuts had bled, they were not the wounds that had killed her. Aunt Cassy had stabbed her in the eye, for like Matilda Drakescourge, Mad Brian Quench, and dozens of other dragon slayers before them, she had known that was a dragon's most vulnerable point. Blinded and helpless, Annacondia had flailed around desperately in darkness, trying to drive away the attacker from her precious egg, while all the time Cassy had slashed at her and taunted her and watched her grow weaker and weaker. Yet though Annacondia had stood up to her attacker, she had not fought back. Queen Dragon knew this, for there were no scorch marks on the walls of the cavern, only some minor burns from Cassy's magic. Confused, Queen Dragon turned to Kniphofia. It was at that point she saw what Kniphofia was weeping over. From beneath the tattered ruin of Annacondia's outflung wing protruded a glistening strip of membrane and a tiny bloodless claw.

Queen Dragon reeled back in horror. Nothing

in all her long life had prepared her for this, had approached the magnitude of Cassy's evil. She uttered a hoarse cry, turned around, and was violently sick.

"Annacondia." A voice spoke in the hatchery entrance. It was so familiar that the sound of it after two thousand years nearly brought Queen Dragon to her knees. She remembered how the voice had whispered to her on the rocks at sunset, like golden honey dripping from a comb, how it had spoken her name and she had trembled with delight. She had been young then, and foolish, but now Queen Dragon saw with a dreadful clarity how hopeless it had always been. King Dragon did not love her. If he had, he would have sought her out, the way she had searched for him. Annacondia was his chosen bride, his wife, his queen. Now she was dead, and Queen Dragon's very presence was an embarrassment. She could not stay here any longer. She could not live with the knowledge of King Dragon's loss.

King Dragon opened his mouth and uttered a terrible cry. It shook the rocks and the surrounding cliffs, and as Kniphofia and the other dragons outside took up the lament, the sound of their harsh keening filled the cave until the air was thick with grief and horror. Queen Dragon knew she should be crying, too, but the sound stuck in her throat. She stared at King Dragon, and as he dropped his ravaged face and looked at her, their eyes met.

Queen Dragon turned and fled.

Lily was standing on the rocks at the aerie's entrance when Queen Dragon came rushing past as if she wasn't there. By the time she had the chance to call out her name, Queen Dragon had flung herself off the rocks into a bank of cloud.

"Queen Dragon! Queen Dragon, come back!" Lily ran to the edge of the cliff. Around her the dragons of Eydelen continued their lament, screaming and flapping their wings in an excess of sorrow. The noise was frightful, wild, and strange to Lily's human ears; it was all she could do not to run away. Most of the dragons were weeping; some looked simply dazed. Then two other dragons emerged from the aerie, a smallish, dumpy red one and King Dragon himself. The screams died away; the flapping stopped. King Dragon pushed through the crowd. He hurried to the edge of the rock and shouted into the wind.

"Sinhault!" His voice went echoing down the valley. "Come back!"

There was no reply. King Dragon gave a harsh cry, hurled himself off the rock into the gathering cloudbank, and disappeared.

"I must go," Lily whispered. "It was a mistake to come. Queen Dragon—she will need me." Underneath the shock, a terrible sense of guilt was welling inside her. Roger and Cassy had somehow followed her and Queen Dragon to Eydelen. Lily was sure of that now, even though she did not know how they had done it. She knew, too, that it had been her own urging that had brought Queen Dragon here in the first place. A wail of grief was building up somewhere inside her, but Lily pushed it down. Her heart was still too full of pain; she could not afford to let it out.

The red dumpy dragon came up to her. "Lily. I am Kniphofia, Sinhault's friend. I think she is now no longer in Eydelen. If you wish to follow her, the magic of the valley will release you. Enter the aerie and keep on walking. The way is dark, but if you want to go it will take you home."

Lily bowed her head. "Thank you."

She took a few steps toward the aerie and paused at the entrance. None of the dragons moved a muscle as she looked back at them. They sat on their rocky perches like so many gargoyles carved from stone. Lily left them and walked swiftly onward. When she reached the hatchery, she paused and forced herself to look at Annacondia's broken body and the ripped and shattered membrane of her egg. It was far worse than she had expected. In that moment, Lily felt something snap inside her and go spinning away. For the first time since the beginning of the world, real loss had come to Eydelen. But something had happened to her as well, and in her heart she knew what it was.

Lily did not linger any longer. She walked on through the cavern and stepped into a passage at the back. The darkness swallowed her up, and she left Eydelen, she hoped, forever.

chapter eight

Rumors of War

Dr. Angela Hartley sat in her old room in the Black Citadel. She was feeling very tired. Ever since the battle she had been working around the clock. Now things in the makeshift hospital were finally starting to calm down. The patients with cuts and bruises and banged heads were getting better, and the ones whose injuries had been going to kill them had, for the most part, died. The two sides, miners and Black Squads, were getting used to working with each other—too used to it, thought Angela as she sipped her tea. The speed with which Gordon had taken control of both the citadel and Manuelo's miners was extremely worrying. And though Gordon had never been anything but kind to her, she could not help being concerned about what he was going to do next.

Angela had lived with Gordon since he'd been a baby. When he'd been only a few months old, a terrible fever had come back to the Black Mountains with one of his father's conquering armies. It had swept through the Black Squads, the mines, and finally through the citadel itself. Gordon's mother had died, and baby Gordon had fallen gravely ill. At that time, Angela had been a slave in the mines, and when the Black Count's doctors had given up on the tiny baby, someone had remembered her existence and called her in. Angela had saved Gordon's life. She had stayed on in the citadel as a doctor and in time had become Gordon's unofficial foster mother. Angela had loved Gordon like her own son. When he had disappeared through the Eye Stone, she had feared that she might never see him again.

Now Gordon was back—but so changed, it was as if he was a different person. It had shocked Angela dreadfully to find him grown up, but discovering how like his father he had become had shocked her even more. He was so polite, so respectful, so considerate, yet so terribly distant it almost broke her heart. Angela did not want this tall, strange young man. She wanted *her* Gordon, the spoiled lonely boy who had come to her for bedtime stories, whom she had comforted when the other boys had rejected him, and whom she had tried to guide in different directions than the ones his father had planned for him. Angela had always hoped she might have made a difference. But her own influence was now too far in the past, and Angela was wise enough to realize that her place in his affections had been taken by someone else. Angela liked Veronica very much. All the same, she did not think it was good for Gordon to have a girlfriend who thought he could do no wrong.

The door opened, and a boy came limping in on crutches. He was pale-faced, plain, and freckled. "Hello, Murdo," said Angela. "How are things going down in the courtyard?"

"They're dividing the troops," Murdo told her. "Half of the army's going to stay here and mind the citadel. The other half's going to Ashby to get rid of Lionel." He sounded extremely pleased about this. Angela, who had saved Murdo's life when he had been a pitiful invalid in the Ashby Hospital, could not help feeling rather annoyed.

"If the Black Army invades Ashby, many people will be killed, Murdo. I suppose you think that's a good thing?"

"That's what soldiers are for," said Murdo. "To die in battle." Something in his voice, though, didn't sound quite as sure as it had the moment before. Angela looked at him sharply.

"What's the matter?"

Murdo did not answer. He fidgeted with his crutches and looked out the window, and, to her astonishment, Angela realized that he was close to tears. Murdo was difficult, suspicious, sometimes cruel. He was not a boy who would easily show someone else how he felt.

"Murdo? What's the matter?"

"She won't let me go," Murdo burst out. "Veronica won't let me go to Ashby with the army. She says I'm too young."

"You *are* too young."

"I'm not too young!" cried Murdo. "It's not fair. If I'd stayed in the past, I could have been in Count Raymond's army with her and Gordon. I'd have been fighting for the last nine years. No one would have said I was too young, then."

"If you'd stayed in the past, you would have been dead," said Angela, but Murdo was not in the mood to listen to reason. He picked up one of his crutches and started smashing at the wall with it. Angela opened her mouth to tell him to stop, then thought better of it. The wall was made out of stone and the crutch was metal. Murdo couldn't hurt either of them, but he was more than capable of hurting himself or her.

"I thought she loved me," he said savagely. "All the time I was in the hospital, she was the only one I thought about. I ran away so I could find her. I knew it was her, even though she was in disguise. And now all she's interested in is *him*, and she won't even let me fight!" The crutch bounced off the wall and went spinning out of his hand. It flew onto the floor and clattered to Angela's feet.

Angela picked it up and spoke very carefully. "Murdo. Are you telling me that Veronica is Manuelo?"

"When it suits her, she is," said Murdo. "They

swap. Sometimes it's Gordon and sometimes it's Veronica. Nobody can tell because of the cape. It means Manuelo can be in more than one place at once."

Angela drew a deep breath. "And you've known this—how long?"

"Ages," said Murdo sullenly. "I guessed. That's why I ran away from Ashby, why I came to the Black Mountains. I knew it had to be Veronica. You see, our father and mother were miners. Our father was called Manuelo."

"Thank you, Murdo," said Angela. "You've been most enlightening." Her hands shook as she handed him back the crutch. Murdo had just given her important information.

The only problem was, she did not know what to do with it.

Lily walked along the passage at the back of the cave for what seemed like a very long way. It was smooth and straight, so that as long as she kept her left hand on the wall she did not stumble in the darkness. After a while the passage started to smell different, and the rock beneath her fingers became smoother and cooler. A small chink of light appeared ahead of her, and she realized she had arrived at a door.

Lily fumbled until she found a catch. She pressed it, and there was a grating sound as a whole section of stonework swung aside. She found herself in a long passageway, painted cream, with several green metal doors on either side of the passage. Lily recognized it immediately. She was in the former dungeons of Ashby Castle, now the treasure vaults that housed the Treasure of Mote Ely. The tunnel out of Eydelen had brought her home.

Quickly, she hurried along the passage and up the stairs. The sentinels at the guard post were surprised to see her, but they knew one another well, and Lily soon passed out through the gatehouse into the castle bailey. Here an unexpected sight met her eyes. Crates and boxes of food and other supplies stood everywhere, stacked underneath tarpaulins; the walls were sandbagged; and trucks drove furiously in and out under the gatehouse. Over by the opposite wall a troop of soldiers was stripping down the cannons from the battlements and cleaning them. Lily was shocked. She had never seen such preparations in the entire time Lionel had been king. She knew they could mean only one thing: Ashby Castle was preparing for war.

"Lily!" Lionel and Evangeline ran down the steps from the South Tower. "We didn't realize you were back!"

"I've only just arrived," said Lily. The king and queen were wearing army combat uniforms, and she could not keep the note of alarm out of her voice. "What's happening?"

"It's a long story," said the king.

"Where's Queen Dragon?" Evangeline asked. Lily shook her head, and immediately their faces fell.

"I'm sorry. Queen Dragon isn't with me. We were traveling separately. I thought—I hoped—she might be with you."

"I'll send a messenger to the dragon house immediately," said the king, beckoning over a guard. "She might be there. Come on, Lily. We've set up my throne room as a war office. I need to fill you in."

The last of the Black Squads had left the citadel and were winding their way down the mountain pass. Gordon sat on his motorbike at the side of the road, watching his army go past. Inside, his stomach was churning. In the last nine years, as a member of Count Raymond's army, he had seen a lot of war. Now he was going into battle on his own, and he was smart enough to realize he was doing everything wrong.

To begin with, nobody wanted to invade Ashby but himself. The miners had mostly never been out of the Black Mountains, and were scared. The professional soldiers knew that winter was the worst possible time to be on the march. It was cold, the supply lines were bad, and there was always the danger of a blizzard coming down from the peaks. There had been mutterings in the ranks and among the officers. Even Veronica was concerned, and though she did not say anything, Gordon knew she did not want to go either. She was worried about her miners, worried about clashes between them and the Black Squads they had been fighting only a week before, and worried about how well an army that had scarcely even trained together would fight. Gordon was anxious about this, too. He was uncertain about leaving the citadel, and he was especially apprehensive about the weather. But he also knew that he could not afford to wait. He had to get his troops down the mountains. He had to get them to Ashby; he had to get rid of Sark. Above all, he had to get the Black Seal.

All day, the army trailed down the road to the foothills of the Black Mountains. About ten o'clock that night the first trucks passed the snow line, and Gordon heaved a sigh of relief. He sent out an order to set up camp and rode his motorbike through the columns of exhausted troops until he reached the head of the army. A sea of tents was already appearing in an open space beside the road. The cold air rang with the sound of hammer blows striking tent pegs.

"Your tent has been pitched, sir."

Gordon gave the motorbike to an aide to take away and strode into his command tent. It was made of the same dark-colored canvas as all the others, though it was bigger, with two rooms inside, one for working and one for sleeping. Oil lamps had been lit, and a small heater was doing its best to warm up the freezing air. Gordon took off his padded gloves and helmet and tossed them in a corner. He was just taking off his leather coat and hanging it on a hook when something, a shadow, seemed to move behind him. Gordon whirled around.

"Who's there?"

No one. Gordon relaxed. The room contained a writing table and chair, dispatch boxes, map cases, and ammunition crates. His duffel bag was in the corner; there was nothing unfamiliar and nowhere to hide. All the same . . . Gordon went over to the canvas partition that separated the main room from the sleeping area and whipped it back. It rasped on its brass rings and revealed a neatly made camp bed, nothing more.

"Good evening, General."

Gordon recognized the voice at once. A prickle of shock ran upward like lightning from the base of his spine. He turned slowly back to the room. A woman with stringy gray hair was sitting at the table, her gnarled hands resting on an unrolled map. Two dark gray eyes looked out of a lined face, and her clothes were dirty and in disarray. Gordon stood staring at her. In his own life, it had been years since he had last seen Aunt Cassy at Mote Ely Castle. In his wildest dreams, he had never expected that he would see her again.

"What—what are you doing here?"

Aunt Cassy glanced down at the map on the table. "If you mean, how did I get here, I came through the Eye Stone at Dragon's Downfall," she said. "There are plenty of them still back in the past, but not so many in this time. Your young friend, Lily Quench, and her dragon friend have been doing their best to close them off. As to *why* I'm here, well, that is rather more complicated."

Gordon stood glued to the spot. Once he had trusted Cassy implicitly. He had believed everything she said, done everything she had suggested—until Lily Quench had arrived at Mote Ely Castle and Cassy's plans and predictions had fallen apart. His eyes fixed on the horrible vial of dragon's blood she wore around her neck, which she had always used to control the Eye Stones. Almost in passing, Gordon noticed that it was full.

"Do you remember the way I told your fortune? How I said you would be a great prince and have your heart's desire?"

"Yes," Gordon answered warily. All the hairs stood up on the back of his neck. He wished Veronica was with him. "I haven't got it yet."

"But you will. That's why I'm here, Gordon. I'm here to help you. I'm here to be at your side when you go in to fight against Lily Quench and her dragon."

Aunt Cassy opened her right hand. A small object was in it, a piece of polished stone like a plumb bob attached to a length of fine silk. She let it drop, and it dangled over the map, one of a series showing the kingdom of Ashby in small detail.

"Let me guide you, Gordon. Let me show you what to do. In return all I ask is a refuge at the citadel—and one other thing."

Gordon wet his lips. A great weight seemed to be pressing down on him, a burden that reached back many years into the past. He found he could not think, that he could barely breathe. A picture flashed into his mind of his father, then his grandfather. He saw the long line of portraits in the gallery of the citadel, all of the Black Counts who had gone before him; he saw blood and fire and iron. Gordon shuddered violently, and his teeth began to chatter. He wanted to say no, to turn away, to escape from whatever it was Cassy had in mind. But then he saw the Black Seal. Its image wavered before his eyes as clearly as if Cassy had been holding it out to him, and somehow, without any effort at all, his mouth opened and the words came out.

"What is it you want?"

Aunt Cassy smiled. "When the fighting is over, I want you to give me Queen Dragon."

Gordon thought of his half-trained, weary army, of the pressing need to get to Ashby and find the seal.

"All right," he said. "What do I have to do?"

chapter nine

The Siege Begins

In the Royal Nursery in Ashby Castle, Queen Evangeline was putting Princess Elizabeth to bed. The baby had been bathed, fed, burped, and changed. Now she was lying in her bassinet, her eyelids drooping. A tiny hand protruded from a pink bunny blanket and wrapped tightly around Evangeline's finger. In the corner a musical lamp played tinkling music and cast a circling pattern of stars, moons, and baby lambs on the wall.

Evangeline lay her head on the side of the bassinet. She breathed in the baby smells of dirty and freshly washed nappies, of talcum powder, soap, and milk. Tears seeped out from under her eyelids. She was very tired. It had been a long day, and there was every chance she would not go to bed again tonight. An hour ago, while she had been feeding the baby, news had arrived that Gordon's army was advancing on Ashby Water. Evangeline was supposed to be up on the battlements, but she did not want to leave. She knew that if she did, there was every chance she would never see her baby again.

Someone tapped gently on the door. Evangeline sat up and drew the blankets over the sleeping princess. She peeped through the heart-shaped cutout in the door and saw Lily Quench standing in the corridor, dressed in her helmet, mail shirt, and fireproof cape. Evangeline had been expecting her. She opened the door.

"Your Majesty?"

"Come in." Evangeline put her finger to her lips to signal she should be quiet. Lily slipped into the room, her chain mail chinking softly. "How is everything going?"

"They expect Gordon's army to arrive in about an hour," Lily whispered. "General Zouche has just sent out some more scouts. We should know more when they get back."

"It'll be tonight, then." Evangeline pushed back her long dark hair and absently secured it with a rubber band. Her leather jerkin was still unbuttoned at the front; she started fastening it up and reached for her coat. "We may not get a chance to speak again, Lily. I'll be honest with you: neither Lionel nor I expect we'll be alive this time tomorrow." She lifted a hand as Lily protested, and went on quietly, "It was always going to be like this. With Queen Dragon we may have stood a chance, but she isn't here. In any case, I didn't become queen of Ashby to prance about in silk dresses. That's not what being queen is all about."

The nursery lamp had stopped tinkling and turning; a lamb was on the floor at Lily's feet. She stared at it numbly while the queen continued.

"I can't say I have no regrets, but I don't have very many. There is only one that matters." Evangeline looked at Lily very steadily. "If the battle starts going against us, as I expect it will, I want you to fetch Elizabeth and take her from the castle. You can leave by the secret passage in the vaults. Escape from Ashby Water, go as far away as you can, and don't come back until Elizabeth is grown up. I mean it, Lily. Your grandmother did as much for Lionel. You must promise not to let us down."

Lily looked at the sleeping baby. "I promise," she said.

"Then everything is ready." Evangeline rang a bell on the wall to summon the baby's nurse. "Come on, Lily. The time has come for Ashby to fight back."

In the castle bailey the final sandbags were being put in place when the first dragonets flew over. Everyone was taken by surprise. A guard patrolling the ramparts on the western wall saw the lights heading for him, aimed his water cannon, and sent up a great spout of Quenching Drops. They missed, and the machines circled over and buzzed off again.

"Hold your fire!" yelled General Zouche from his command post near the North Tower. "You twit! Don't you know those drops are in short supply? Fire them when you've got a chance of hitting something, you great drongo!" He stamped down the stairs, and from the courtyard King Lionel and Mr. Hartley heard him rousing on the hapless guards.

"Some things about Zouche have never changed," said the king wryly.

"He's certainly better at organizing troops than he was my parishioners," said Mr. Hartley. "When he was helping at the church, there were plenty of times I had to bite my tongue."

"Oddly enough, I think Zouche was probably always quite a good soldier," said Lionel. "It was the day-to-day governing of Ashby he was so hopeless at. Here's Lily. Shall we do the inspection?" He opened the door of a battered truck that was parked nearby and gave Lily a leg up into the bed. Mr. Hartley got into the passenger seat, and they drove out under the open portcullis into the town.

The streets of Ashby Water were strangely deserted as they rattled along. Lionel drove fast, and Lily had to hold on tightly to stop herself from sliding around. If she had not known it was Ashby Water, she would have scarcely recognized the barricaded streets and sandbagged buildings.

All the windows of the houses were taped up and lined with black paper so that no one could see if there was anyone inside. Their doors were locked and bolted, and their fires were out. There were no pedestrians and no vehicles, except the odd truck carrying volunteer fighters to the barricades. They waved as they saw Lionel drive by and shouted, "Ashby forever!" The drivers blew their horns and flashed their lights. Lionel tooted back to them, and Lily waved enthusiastically from the back of the truck.

The king leaned out of the window. "We're going to the church," he shouted to Lily. "The tower will be a good vantage point." He pulled in through the gates and parked in the carpark. Mr. Hartley opened the belltower door with a key, and the three of them climbed the stairs to the top of the tower.

Lily had not been inside the tower since the battle that had restored Lionel to his throne. Then it had been full of dust and pigeon droppings, but volunteer workers had since cleaned it up and replaced the broken steps, and it was altogether a more cheerful and less threatening place. At length they came out onto a viewing platform, from which the whole of Ashby Water could be seen stretched out like a map. Lionel pointed with his unlit flashlight at a dark mass on the western outskirts of the town. It spread across the road from the canal to Ashby Thicket. It was the first time Lily had ever seen an army in the field. The sheer size of it made her practically give up there and then.

"There they are," said the king. "The Black Army. Now I know how my father felt all those years ago at the Siege of Ashby."

Lily swallowed. The fact that it was night and she could not make out much more than the army's dark bulk made the sight only more sinister. Ranged against them on the roads leading into the town were General Zouche's barricades, manned by volunteers armed with Quenching Drops. Their preparations seemed unbelievably inadequate, and for all her Quench blood and experience, Lily felt small and inadequate, too. It occurred to her that, in all her adventures, she had never actually used the sword that hung at her belt. All the battles she had been involved in had been struggles of courage, wits, and endurance. When strength and fighting ability had been needed, Queen Dragon had always been there to provide them. Until now. Since her return to Ashby Water, Lily had hoped against hope that Queen Dragon would reappear. But she hadn't, and there was no escaping the unpleasant reality that Lily would have to fight Ashby's final battle by herself.

The air vibrated, and the vibrations grew louder until they became a menacing buzz. Bright lights were sweeping over the roofs of the houses, heading toward the church.

"Here come the dragonets again," said Lionel. "Time to get out, I think. Quickly, Lily. Downstairs to the truck."

"The first ones didn't do any damage," Lily began, and then her words were cut off by a flash and a thundering explosion. The tower rocked. Lily flung herself down and flinched as dirt and pebbles showered over her. The air was filled with evil-smelling smoke.

"Not this time," said Lionel. "I think Gordon's reconnaissance is over."

Down on the banks of the Ashby Canal, on the outskirts of the town, three hooded figures stood looking at the water. It was dark, and its surface was flecked with a few drops of rain. The current flowed steadily downhill toward Ashby Water, its castle, and the sea.

A tangle of bushes hid them from the rest of the army, and guards had been posted to make sure they were not interrupted. Gordon was glad of that. He felt vaguely uncertain about what they were doing and did not want anyone else to see. Beside him Veronica watched without comment as Aunt Cassy took a flask from beneath her cloak and removed its stopper. She marched up the steps onto a nearby lock and tipped it sideways over the railing. Its contents poured into the water like oily syrup, making no sound as it hit the surface of the canal.

Gordon had not realized he had been holding his breath. He exhaled and walked over to the edge of the canal so he could peer in. The liquid from the flask was floating on the surface in an iridescent slick. As he and Veronica watched, Aunt Cassy put her hand into her cloak and drew out the small stone she'd had with her in Gordon's campaign tent. She leaned over the railing and gently let it down on its silken string. When it was dangling like a pendulum just above the surface of the slick, she stopped. Slowly, very slowly, the liquid began to move.

Like creeping fingers, it flowed along the surface of the canal. Small green and blue flames leapt up like flambé on a Christmas pudding, casting eerie reflections on the surface of the water. The flames burned and spread, flowing downstream from the lock, growing bigger and stronger until the entire surface of the canal seemed to be ablaze.

Aunt Cassy remained motionless, leaning over the railing. Her eyes were closed, and the pendulum moved imperceptibly in her fingers, directing the flow of the magic. Gordon felt Veronica's hand reach out for his. Neither of them were nervous people, but tonight their fingers silently linked in hope and fear.

They were thinking of the people in Ashby Water, as Aunt Cassy sent her green fire down on their unsuspecting town.

chapter ten

Green Fire

King Lionel put his foot down on the accelerator and the truck leapt out through the church gates and roared down the street. Lily held on for dear life. The air was filled with smoke and dust and the chemical scent of explosives.

"I think they're aiming at the castle," Mr. Hartley shouted. "The bomb that landed in the church grounds must have been a mistake."

"Dragonets are a relatively new invention," said Lionel, turning a corner. "I imagine the pilots haven't had much practice." He jammed his foot on the brake, and the car screeched to a halt. Lily slewed around violently in the truck bed, her mail shirt rattling against the metal like a dropped bag of nails. Breathlessly, she sat up and straightened her helmet. A strange greenish fire was burning in the street ahead of them, the flames as high as the buildings lining the road.

"It must be some sort of chemical from the bombs," said Lionel, after the three of them had sat, staring at it for a moment. "Sorry, Lily. Are you all right?" He waited until Lily had rearranged her fireproof cape, then turned the truck around and drove off in the opposite direction. The smoke thickened around them, and Lily began to choke and cough. Her eyes watered. They drove past several smaller fires, including two at barricades, then were stopped near the town hall by another large blaze in the roadway.

"This is really strange," said Lionel. "I've never seen fire like that." He and Mr. Hartley got out of the truck, and Lily stood up in the back. The sky around them was drenched with eerie light, like evening mist in a rain forest. Green fires had sprung up all over Ashby Water and were spreading even as they watched. A few tiny flames, tinged with blue and purple, licked the pavement at Lionel's feet, then shot off along the gutters as if they were alive.

Mr. Hartley stamped one experimentally with his boot. It did not extinguish, and when he tried again, it jumped away from him. "This is no natural fire," he said. "This is magic."

"Look! The town hall is burning!" At the end of the street, the town hall clock tower was ablaze with a ghostly green light. As Lily pointed, the dragon weathervane broke away from its fastenings, veered over, and toppled with an enormous crash onto the street.

"Main roads and public buildings," said Lionel. "That's what he's targeting. Gordon's crippling the town before he even sets foot in it. But how's he doing it? *Who* is doing it? And how are we going to stop them?"

The treasure vaults were unusually quiet that night. In his cell in the old Ashby Castle dungeons, General Sark strained his ears for the sound of metal doors clanging open and shut, of guards walking up and down the corridors. But there was nothing. Even the rumble of traffic through the gatehouse overhead had stopped.

The general picked up a magazine from the pile they had given him and started flicking idly through it. Halfway through a nauseating article on the new Royal Infant, he became aware of a scratching noise. It sounded like a rat in the corridor and at first he ignored it, but the noise persisted and when he put down his magazine and went tiptoeing to the door, he clearly heard that it was coming from the lock. The fact that someone was trying to break into his cell was either a good sign or a very bad one. Anyone who had a right to be there should have been opening the door with a key.

There was a click as the lock disengaged. The general lifted his hands and dropped into a karate stance.

"Eeeeeeey-aaahh!"

The door swung open. As the general launched himself at the two people standing in the outside corridor, they screamed and jumped. He cannoned into them and the three of them hit the floor in a bone-crunching tangle. Sark glimpsed a bearded man and a female body in a fur-trimmed jumpsuit. With a cry of loathing, he shoved the woman roughly aside and stood up.

"You!" Sark exclaimed. He quickly straightened his uniform. "Crystal Bright! What are *you* doing here?"

"I could ask the same of *you*." Queen Evangeline's mother pushed her purple hair back into place. "It's taken Patterson twenty minutes to pick that lock. We were expecting bags of treasure, not a worn-out old traitor."

Sark was annoyed. He had always prided himself on looking extremely youthful for his age, and since Crystal had already made one attempt to sell Ashby to the Black Empire, he considered she had no right to call anyone a traitor. He looked at the man who was with her and realized that he was familiar, too. Patterson was a thief who had plagued the Black Citadel for years. In Sark's opinion, relieving the Black Empire of his presence was the best thing Lionel of Ashby had ever done.

"Depends on your point of view," he retorted. "What's this treasure you're talking about? Something you're looking to steal, no doubt."

"Steal?" said Patterson innocently. "Not at all. We were just on our way out."

"Your way out? Down here? Do you think I'm a fool?"

"As a matter of fact, there's a secret tunnel under the castle walls," said Crystal. "Things were getting a trifle hot up there, and we thought it was time to leave. Sorry to disturb you, Sarkie. We'll just close you up again and be on our way."

"Close me up?" Sark took an angry step toward them. "Come on, Crystal. You can't intend to leave me here."

"Why not?" returned Crystal. "What have you ever done for me?"

"At the moment I could do rather a lot," snapped Sark. "At least I'm a trained general, unlike Lionel the Librarian. He's having a hard time of it up there, isn't he? His castle's surrounded; Gordon's troops are pressing him hard. Well, how about letting me out so I can fight them? I couldn't do a worse job of defending Ashby than your drippy son-in-law."

Crystal stared at him incredulously. "You want me to let *you* fight Gordon?"

"Why not? I want to get rid of the little twerp as much as you do."

Crystal and Patterson exchanged doubtful glances.

"Well," said Crystal, "I suppose it's a thought. Things couldn't possibly go worse than they're going now. Evangeline has to stay queen of Ashby, though," she added conscientiously. "I am her mother, after all. I wouldn't like to let her down."

"I couldn't give a rap about Ashby," said Sark. "It was always more trouble than it was worth. You can do what you like with it. What about the Black Seal?"

"Yours, if you want it," said Crystal. "A deal?"

"A deal," said Sark, and he held out his hand. *Payback at last*, he thought, as Crystal shook it. He knew she was lying as she always did, but this time, so was he.

The moat was filled with green flame when the king's truck arrived back outside Ashby Castle. Lionel put his hand down on the horn, the portcullis went up, and he gunned the truck across the drawbridge and under the gatehouse. Lily felt tongues of flame briefly lick her fire-proof cape, then the drawbridge was going up behind them and they were safe.

The king killed the engine and got out of the cab. Bombs were falling around the castle, and the sound of approaching dragonets was deafening. Up on the ramparts, Queen Evangeline waved and started running down the stairs.

"Thank goodness you're back!" The queen hugged Lionel and gave him a kiss. Her face was streaked with dirt and tears. "I thought you must have been trapped out there. Lionel, there are strange fires all over the castle. We can't put them out. What on earth is happening?"

"I'm not sure exactly." A gush of green fire leapt up behind a mound of sandbags as the king spoke. More bombs exploded, and there was a shout of "Fire!" from the western wall. The king started moving swiftly toward the stairs. The others followed him all the way up to the ramparts. When they reached the top, Lily looked over the battlements and froze. Green fire filled the streets of Ashby Water, while on the town's perimeter a dark mass of troops, tanks, and trucks was moving relentlessly into the outer suburbs.

"Look at what the fires are doing." Mr. Hartley pointed. "They're cutting our defenders off, but moving back and opening up gaps to let Gordon's troops come through. No natural fire burns like that. Gordon's using magic to hole us up while he comes to get us."

"This was the stretch of wall my father fell from in the last siege," said Lionel quietly.

"I know," said Mr. Hartley. "I was there."

Lily said nothing. Her own father, Godfrey Quench, had also been there with King Alwyn the Last on that dreadful day, but unlike Mr. Hartley, he had not survived. Black Squad troops had shot him down; he had fallen into the moat, and his body had never been recovered. Lily felt her heart curl around the edges like a burned piece of paper. The king and queen were standing silently, hand in hand. The king looked at Mr. Hartley and nodded curtly, and then quite suddenly tears welled up in Evangeline's eyes. She looked at Lily imploringly, then turned and buried her face in Lionel's neck.

"Come on, Lily," said Mr. Hartley. "You know what you have to do. I'll come with you part of the way." He took her hand, and they started walking along the ramparts, but Lily could not help looking back over her shoulder. She saw the king and queen standing slumped in each other's arms, and suddenly her own tears could no longer be contained. They splashed down her cheeks until she could hardly see where she was putting her feet. She stumbled and, if Mr. Hartley had not caught her, would have fallen down the steps.

"Watch it!" Mr. Hartley produced a handkerchief. Lily took it and mopped her face. She still felt terrible, but now she was embarrassed as well. The king and queen were relying on her to save the princess, and here she was crying like a baby herself! Trying hard to feel more like a Quench, Lily followed Mr. Hartley through a door into the west wing of the castle. They passed swiftly along a deserted corridor, past offices and rooms allocated to palace staff. Outside the green flames roared against the narrow windows, giving everything a curious undersea glow. The green fire did not seem to consume what it touched, but the noise and heat were fearful. Lily could see paint blistering on the walls, while furniture smoked and carpets and curtains smoldered and burst into real flame.

Lily pulled her fireproof cape tightly around her. Mr. Hartley had no such protection, but the heat did not deter him, and though several times

Lily thought they must turn back, he hurried her on from room to room. The faster they ran, the higher the fires seemed to surge. They turned a corner and suddenly everything came crashing down around them.

"The roof!" Lily screamed and wrapped her arms around her head. The ceiling above them had collapsed. Burning wood and rubble went crashing through the wooden floor in front of them, and everything was suddenly flame and smoke so that she could scarcely see. The floor shifted under Lily's feet, and she went staggering backward. Behind them more flames were surging through the open doorway, the real fires mingling with the magic ones. It was hard to tell which were the more terrifying. "We're being cut off!"

Mr. Hartley nodded, though Lily knew he could not possibly have heard what she had said. The sound of the fire, the falling debris, and the bombs still raining down outside made her feel as if the world was ending all around her. Mr. Hartley grabbed her hand and drew her forward, closer to the inferno. Lily yelled and struggled, then looked into the glowing heart and saw to her combined horror and amazement that the central beam that had supported the broken floor was still in place.

"I can't! *I can't!*"

"You can!" Mr. Hartley stepped out onto the beam, giving Lily no choice but to follow him. The beam rocked and wobbled under her feet; she saw Mr. Hartley mouthing words of encouragement, and then he let go of her hand and started walking along the beam in front of her. Lily closed her eyes. Her very eyelashes seemed to singe beneath her fireproof cape, her skirts were smoking, and she felt her feet burning in their thick leather-soled boots so that she could barely keep her balance. In her mind's eye she seemed to see a face. Aunt Cassy was sitting at a folding table in what looked like a tent, dangling an object like a yo-yo from her fingers. She was moving it slowly, deliberately over a map of Ashby Water, directing the green fire through the streets toward the castle.

"Stop it!" Lily shouted at the picture in her head. "You have no right to do this to me!" The image abruptly vanished, and Lily opened her eyes. Mr. Hartley was looking at her from halfway across the beam, and she realized she must have spoken aloud.

The horrible greedy flames, green and gold intermingled, reached up around their ankles, but somehow they now seemed less dreadful. Lily lifted her arms up to balance herself and took a step forward, then another and another. The beam shifted and creaked, but Lily kept her mind on what she was doing, and her eyes on Mr. Hartley. Light as a cat on a rickety fence, he walked to the very end of the beam and jumped onto the narrow ledge of remaining stonework. Lily followed him. As she landed on the solid ledge, the wooden beam gave a sudden lurch behind her and fell away.

Mr. Hartley grabbed a piece of burning wood from the floor and smashed at a door in the stonework. It flew open, and a moment later he and Lily were standing in a familiar stairwell. There was no fire there, no smoke; the flames had stopped mysteriously at the very threshold. They were in the South Tower at last, and a few steps brought them to the door of the baby princess's room.

Mr. Hartley put his hand in his pocket and pressed something into Lily's palm.

"You'll need this to get out of the secret

passage, Lily. It's the key to the church crypt. Good-bye, and good luck."

"Good luck to you, too." Lily knocked on the nursery door. The princess's nurse opened it, and a moment later she was safe inside.

Mr. Hartley continued quickly on his way. The king's private sitting room was one floor down, and he took the steps two at a time and unlocked its door with the key Lionel had given him. Inside, in a locked cupboard was the leather bag the king had told him to look for. Mr. Hartley briefly undid the drawstring and half tipped the object inside onto his palm. The Black Seal flickered in his torchlight. Mr. Hartley dropped it in his pocket and hurried down the king's private staircase to the library.

As he stepped into the room something moved on the floor in front of him. A sweat broke out on Mr. Hartley's forehead, and he stopped dead in his tracks.

Sitting in the middle of the library floor was a rat.

From the castle ramparts, Lionel and Evangeline saw Lily's doughty little figure emerge from the foot of the South Tower. Nestled under her fireproof cape was a telltale bulge: their precious daughter, wrapped in blankets and carried in her sling.

"Thank goodness," said Lionel, as Lily disappeared into the gatehouse. "At least they're going to be safe." He stared out over Ashby Water, at the armies gathered to destroy what was left of his kingdom. This time tomorrow, it would all be over. This time tomorrow, Ashby would again be part of the Black Empire and he and Evangeline would be dead.

The buzz of engines sounded deafeningly overhead: another flight of dragonets was attacking the castle. There was a rattling sound as the Quenching Machines fired off another round of drops. One of the dragonets peeled off from the formation, and at first Lionel thought that it had been hit. It hurtled down toward the South Tower, pulled up at the last moment, and landed. Two black-clad figures jumped down from the cockpit. They swung a ladder over the top of the tower and started climbing nimbly down its darkened wall. A stray Quenching Drop hit the abandoned dragonet, and it creaked loudly and started falling apart.

"What on earth are they doing?" Evangeline stared at the climbing figures. They reached a window, kicked it in, and disappeared inside the tower.

"It's Gordon, of course," said Lionel. "Now we know why the South Tower isn't burning. He's come to get the seal."

Lily unlatched the door to the secret tunnel. She switched on the flashlight she had brought with her and crept through the gap. It was darker than she remembered, and the passage was cold and smelled awful. Lily closed the door behind her. In the sling against her heart, Elizabeth slept on.

It was several minutes' walk from the castle to the church. From time to time Lily heard muffled noises that she guessed were bombs, but the passage was too strong and too deeply built to be affected by them. At the end of the passage was a flight of steps. Lily released a second catch and a stone swung aside, so that she emerged into a low, vaulted chamber, filled with tombs. Lily did not linger but unlocked the security grille at the end of the room with the key Mr. Hartley had given her. A few minutes later she was standing at the foot of the tower, unlatching the same small door she and her friends had used earlier that evening.

The baby stirred against her chest and made a little noise, half squeak, half sigh. Lily paused to adjust Elizabeth's wooly bonnet against the cold night air and stepped cautiously out into the carpark. Her flashlight beam glanced off something enormous, bright, and golden, and she screamed aloud.

It was King Dragon.

chapter eleven

The Black Seal

In the darkness of the Southern Ocean, a rocky island rose above the waves. It was a volcano, a craggy remnant of some ancient undersea eruption. Thick rain poured down on it, hissing as it passed over hot spots in the rock and running in dirty sheets down into the crater. From time to time a flash of lightning illuminated a shingly beach. On the shingle, wet, abandoned, and unhappy, lay Queen Dragon.

Queen Dragon stared out across the crater. Once upon a time, she had liked to bathe in its mud pool. Once upon a time, this volcano had been her home. It did not seem to be that any longer. The worst part of finding Eydelen, Queen Dragon thought, was that now she had been there she would never be truly happy anywhere else. She had lived beneath the volcano for more than seven hundred years, and it had always seemed like a refuge. But when Eydelen's magic had sent her home to it, there had been no solace in returning there, no sense of homecoming, no peace.

Queen Dragon wept. She had thought all her tears were long since cried out, but somehow she kept finding more to shed. What was left for her now but to sit on this beach, eating gold out of her treasure piles and wondering when her life was going to end? There was nobody to see her, nobody to care. She had no fiancé, no Eydelen to dream about in the darkness, no dragon friends to help or console her. Even Lily was no longer at her side. Queen Dragon hoped Lily had found her way back to Ashby Water. She knew Lily would miss her, but eventually she would learn to be happy without her. And that, of course, was the whole problem. Lily was more like a dragon than any other human Queen Dragon had ever met, but she was still a human. With dreadful clarity, Queen Dragon saw that human love, valuable though it was, was not enough. She needed the friendship of other dragons, the love and companionship of her own kind that could endure for thousands of years without breaking or betrayal; a love that understood without explanation who she was and what she yearned for. For years just the hope of this had sustained her, but now Queen Dragon needed more. A dreadful compulsion seized her, a driving urge that stiffened her body and fired her resolve. Queen Dragon lifted her scaly face to the heavens. The rain beat down on it, washing away her tears.

"Lily," whispered Queen Dragon. "I'm so sorry."

She left the shingle and started clawing her way up the rocks to the volcano's summit.

Mr. Hartley stood looking at the rat on the library floor. It was ludicrous, he knew, to be so scared of such a tiny thing. Ordinarily he was far from being a coward. He had been present at the first Siege of Ashby, had endured years of exile and hardship. But all that had been nothing compared to this. Mr. Hartley had been terrified of rats for so long he no longer remembered why.

The rat twitched its whiskers. Mr. Hartley felt the hairs on the back of his neck stand on end. *It was not even a very big rat*, he told himself. It was probably as scared as he was. He closed his eyes and prayed. Every muscle in his body seemed to tremble. Mr. Hartley took a tiny step forward. Suddenly the rat scuttled toward him and shot between his legs. Mr. Hartley yelled at the top of his lungs, staggered back against a bookcase, and almost fainted.

"Good evening," said a voice. "Is something the matter?"

Mr. Hartley clung tightly to the bookcase. A few books fell off a shelf and landed at his feet. He picked them up and shoved them back among the other titles, higgledy-piggledy. The voice repeated the question, and this time Mr. Hartley recovered enough to turn in the direction it had come from. Standing in front of the library window, gently backlit by the green fires in the courtyard, was a young dark-haired man. A girl crouched on the windowsill behind him. Both of them were wearing black combat clothes with knives in their belts and bandoliers slung over their shoulders.

"Perhaps you don't remember me," said the young man politely. "We never had a chance to speak personally back at the citadel, and I realize I've probably changed quite a lot since you last saw me. My name is Gordon. We last met at Dragon's Downfall, the day my father died."

"Yes. I remember." Now that the rat had vanished, Mr. Hartley was recovering his courage. "I remember you, too, Gordon. Why are you here?"

"You have something I want."

"Do I?"

"I believe so. Cassy told me the Black Seal was in Lionel's sitting room upstairs, and there's something heavy in your jacket pocket. I'm afraid I'm not going to let you leave this room until I have it."

"I would hardly hand it over just because you asked me to."

"There are two of us," Gordon pointed out. "I know you're stronger than you look, but Veronica and I are soldiers. You must be at least forty—"

"Forty-two," admitted Mr. Hartley.

"—and the two of us could quite easily overpower you. We'd try not to kill you, but it would be extremely unpleasant, and in the end, we'd get what we wanted anyway. It would be much better for everyone if you just handed it over now."

"I'm sure it would be," said Mr. Hartley. "But I'm afraid I'm not going to. If you want the seal, Gordon, you might as well kill me now. It's what your father would have done, after all."

An ugly flush spread over Gordon's face. "Don't mention my father. He's dead. It's me you're dealing with now, not him."

"Is it?" Mr. Hartley returned. "He's the reason you're here, isn't he? It's his empire you want to reclaim. All this—" he gestured to the magical flames licking up at the library window "—is directed at one thing. The recovery of your father's empire and the transfer of his power to yourself. I'm sure you're brave and clever enough to do it. You've gotten this far, after all. All that remains to be seen is how much of a Black Count you really are—and how much you want to become your father."

Veronica jumped down off the windowsill and laid a warning hand on Gordon's arm. But it was unnecessary. "I thought I did want to become my father," said Gordon unexpectedly. "I thought it for a long time. It was why I went back into the past. I tried to build up an army, but I was too young, and it didn't work. So Veronica and I joined Count Raymond's army instead."

Veronica's fingers tightened. Gordon knew she was remembering Raymond. It was a sobering thought. Count Raymond had been an animal, a man who killed and rampaged and enslaved without pity or remorse, who had believed himself invincible until Gordon himself, his trusted lieutenant in many battles, had unexpectedly challenged and betrayed him. Suddenly, Gordon found he was asking himself an uncomfortable question: *Why* had he done that? When Raymond had announced he was invading Ashby all those centuries ago, why had he and Veronica cut off the army's supply lines and stopped him? Gordon had told himself that it was because the conquest of Ashby rightly belonged to him and to his father, but now, looking at Angela's husband standing before him, he was not so sure. If he had never met Lily Quench in the snow outside the citadel, would he have even bothered? And what about the miners? If he had never seen

Angela trudging down to the encampments with her doctor's bag, would he have cared enough to become Manuelo and set them free to fight against Sark?

"We couldn't stay in the past," he said aloud. "It doesn't matter why. Veronica and I used the Eye Stone to travel forward into this time. We knew the miners would fight against Sark if only someone would organize them. I was trying to help them, you know. I thought, if only they will fight for me, I will set them free. The Black Counts don't have to be like Raymond. They don't even have to be like my father. I thought that things could change."

"You're right, they can," said Mr. Hartley. "But not unless people change, too. You haven't changed enough, Gordon. Trying to do things differently is putting the cart before the horse. You need to start again from the very beginning. And to do that, you cannot be the Black Count. You have to renounce that heritage."

"No!" Gordon cried. "I loved my father! I tried everything I could to please him. It was my fault that he died. How can you ask me to do that?"

"I would not have you do anything but love

your father," said Mr. Hartley steadily. "I certainly know he loved you more than anything in his entire empire. But you must love him and know what he was, without lies or equivocation, and you must understand what the inheritance he left you is. If you choose to embrace it, I cannot stop you. You can become Black Count, you can wade in blood, you can grind Ashby and every other kingdom east of the mountains under your booted foot. You can even try to change things, though I doubt in the end that you will be able to. For the bloodline of the Black Counts is an inheritance of death and fear and destruction, and it will come to you as inevitably as the sun will come up tomorrow morning. You cannot change that, Gordon. But you do have a chance to stop it."

Mr. Hartley put his hand in his jacket pocket and tossed the seal, in its leather pouch, onto the library table. It landed on the wood with a little thud. "I think this is what you are looking for. I don't much fancy being attacked or set on and beaten. It's yours. It's up to you now to decide what you're going to do with it."

Gordon picked up the seal. He remembered it from his childhood when it had nestled in its black leather pouch in a drawer of his father's desk. No one would have dared touch it then. He himself would not have seen it more than three or four times in his entire life. Gordon knew that he had failed in even allowing Sark to walk away with so precious a talisman. But now the seal had come back to him, and it was all worth it: the battles, the bloodshed, Manuelo, even Aunt Cassy and her horrible magic. Gordon opened the pouch and slowly tipped the seal onto his palm. It was black and flawless, with a red tinge in its heart. For a moment as he stared into its depths it reminded Gordon unaccountably of Aunt Cassy, sitting in his campaign tent with her map and pendulum, and then there was a wrench in his head as if something was pulling his thoughts back in a different direction. The seal was his. He could do whatever he wanted with it.

He *was* the Black Count.

"There is bad magic afoot tonight," said King Dragon. He lifted his golden face to the night air. It was as if he could smell it. "I had not expected this when I came here. Something is very wrong."

"The town and castle are being attacked," said Lily. "They are about to fall to our enemies. The king and queen sent me out of the castle to save their baby. You're lucky to have found me."

"And Sinhault?" said King Dragon. "Where is she? I thought—I hoped—she would be here."

"I don't know where she is," said Lily. "I thought she must still be somewhere in Eydelen."

King Dragon shook his head. "A thousand years have passed in Eydelen since I saw you there. In all that time I have never once laid eyes on Sinhault. I came here to Ashby to seek her out."

"A thousand years?" Lily stared at him. "It's only been a couple of days here. How can it possibly be a thousand years since I saw you?"

"In places like Eydelen, time flows differently than in the ordinary world," said King Dragon. "Just as you can jump out of Eydelen into any place, you can leave it to go into any time. But I see I have made a mistake. I asked the magic to release me to Sinhault's home, and it sent me here."

"This is Queen Dragon's home," said Lily. "Part of the time, at any rate. She has another one in a volcano, across the ocean. Perhaps she is there."

"Then I must leave at once," said King Dragon. "Farewell, Lily. I am sorry to have troubled you." He turned and lifted his wings to spring into the air. Lily ran across the asphalt after him.

"No! Wait!" she cried. As she spoke there was a huge crash from the castle. Repeated bombing had hit a weak spot in the stonework and brought down a large section of wall. "The magic—it's Aunt Cassy, the magician who killed Annacondia. Don't you see? If we don't stop her now, Ashby will fall and none of us will be safe, humans or dragons. The castle walls are breached! We can't just leave the people in there to die!"

"I cannot help them," said King Dragon. "To do so, I would have to harm or kill. I cannot betray my vows."

"If you do nothing, people are going to die anyway," said Lily passionately. "You'll be responsible for that, as much as if you flamed someone. And then, when Ashby falls, Aunt Cassy will follow you back to Eydelen. She will kill and imprison the dragons. You saw what she did to Annacondia. If you don't fight back now, you will be finished!"

"I know that," said King Dragon. "Believe me,

Lily, I know it better than you could imagine. But I cannot help it, either. All I can say is that if you had been at the Great War of the Dragons you would understand." He looked up suddenly. Above the sound of the dragonets and falling bombs, the marching feet of Gordon's soldiers could be heard advancing down the roadways to the castle. Dismayed, Lily realized she had stayed too long in talking. The way out of Ashby Water was now blocked off: she and Elizabeth would never escape.

"What's that noise?" King Dragon whispered. His golden ears were lifted like a dog's, and he was listening intently, not to the sounds of battle, but to something farther off. "It sounds—it sounds like a dragon."

"There are no dragons—" Lily began, and then suddenly she heard it, too. Not in her human ears, but in the quiet places of her heart, an anguished cry was ringing in a familiar voice, a cry for help and love.

King Dragon's golden scales had lost their color. "It's the Dragon's Cry of Summoning. I think—I think it's Sinhault."

chapter twelve

Queen Dragon's Cry

Lily's arms tightened instinctively around the sleeping princess. "The Cry of Summoning? She can't! If Queen Dragon's in her volcano, there'll be no other dragons anywhere near her. The cry will turn back on her. It will kill her!"

"She's a very long way off," said King Dragon, listening intently. "I can barely hear her, and my ears are keener than most dragons. But it *is* Sinhault. I would always hear her voice if she was in need."

"I can only hear her in my heart," said Lily. "What can we do?"

"We must answer the cry at once and hope she can hear us," said King Dragon. He closed his eyes, threw back his head, and began to sing.

Lily knew that among dragonkind King Dragon's songs were famous. She had heard them sung by other dragons, including Queen Dragon herself; she had even heard snippets of his own singing in the cave in Eydelen. But this was different. Tonight, King Dragon was singing for Queen Dragon's life. As the first notes flowed from his open mouth, the buildings around them trembled to their foundations. The sky above Ashby was rent by golden lightning. Lily dropped to her knees, and Princess Elizabeth woke up and looked out from under her pink woolen bonnet. In Gordon's campaign tent, Cassy dropped her pendulum and knocked over the table. The green fire in the streets of Ashby Water flickered and went out; the advancing soldiers broke ranks and scattered. On the steps of the South Tower of Ashby Castle, Sark, Patterson, and Crystal paused, then staggered in through the broken door.

Buildings crashed down, dragonets went spinning out of control. Trees shivered in Ashby Thicket, and in the caves in the Ashby Hills, Jason Pearl and his refugees cried out in fear and wonder. King Dragon's song of love and hope shook Ashby Water to its core, but still it was not enough.

"She's too far away!" gasped King Dragon. His eyes were bulging with the effort of maintaining the song; the scales on his chest and back turned glassy white and fell in tinkling showers on the ground. "She can't hear me! The Cry of Summoning. It's turning back on her! Lily, it's too late!"

"Queen Dragon!" Lily shouted. "Can you hear me? It's me, Lily! Hold on! Don't let go! Hold on! *Hold on!*" All at once everything Lily had ever felt for Queen Dragon, all the companionship and friendship and love, rushed up and poured, unbidden, from her heart. "Queen Dragon!" Together their two voices went winging out across the ocean, riding the waves like seagulls. Suddenly, Lily saw Queen Dragon. She was standing on the top of her volcano, looking out across the sea, and the Cry of Summoning was starting to turn back on her. Lily could see the hopelessness in her eyes, her drooping body. *Hold on, Queen Dragon,* she willed her. *Hold on.* Queen Dragon started, as if she had heard her, and then, somewhere over the water, King Dragon's song hit the sound of Queen Dragon's cry.

"Sinhault!"

"King Dragon!" Lily heard a faint but strangled cry, and then, *"Oh, my love, my love!"* As the sound of hysterical, happy weeping filled her head, Lily's own eyes filled with tears. Queen Dragon was safe. But in the thrill of her rescue, she had not so much as mentioned Lily's name.

Crystal ran hoppity-skip up the stairs of the South Tower. It was totally dark, and she had wrenched her foot. She didn't like running, and she especially didn't like running after General Sark. "You no-good scum!" she yelled as she limped along. "You said you were going to fight Gordon for me. What are you doing in here, you coward? You're no better than that louse, Lionel! Why, you're no better than *Patterson.*"

"I heard that!" said a voice behind her.

"Shut up."

"No. You shut up."

"The Black Seal!" panted Sark. "I have to get it!"

"You don't even know it's in here," protested Patterson.

"Of course it's here," snapped Crystal. "Lionel keeps all his important stuff in this tower. What I want to know is what *he* wants it for?"

"To stop Gordon's army, of course, you stupid old bag," snarled Sark. "Now, where's this Royal Sitting Room? Or do I have to tear this tower down, piece by piece?"

Crystal pointed to the library door. Sark fumbled with the lock, then drew the gun he had picked up in the bailey and blasted it open. The people in the room jumped aside as Sark came crashing through the door and fired again into the ceiling. Crystal shrieked.

"Stop right there!" roared Sark. "Or I'll shoot you dead, all of you!"

As the door exploded inward, Gordon's fingers instinctively tightened around the seal. Of all the people he had expected to appear, Sark was both the least and most likely. It was Sark, after all, who had started everything; Sark, who had usurped his father; Sark, who had stolen the Black Seal and caused this invasion. All the pain and hardship Gordon had endured since his father had died and he had jumped through the Eye Stone could be laid to Sark's account. At the sight of his enemy he felt a black knot of hatred tighten around his heart.

Faster than anyone could see, Veronica whipped a knife out of her boot. If she'd had the chance to throw it, everything would have been over, for she never missed; but Sark's finger was already on the trigger of his gun. He jerked around and fired. The bullet hit Veronica in the shoulder, and she staggered back into a bookcase and slumped to the floor.

Everyone screamed. Sark's companions dived onto the floor, Gordon yelled and flung himself at Veronica, and Mr. Hartley sprang toward Gordon and wrenched him back just in time. Sark's gun went off again, and the bullet whistled past Gordon's ear and buried itself in a wall. Angrily, Gordon shoved Mr. Hartley away. In that second, Sark was in front of him, and the gun was leveled at his chest.

"Give me the seal."

"Let me see to Veronica," said Gordon.

"She stays where she is," said Sark. "Give me the seal."

"Let me see to her!" If he had not been holding

the Black Seal, Gordon would have knocked the general down without a thought. He did not care about being shot himself and had been in more dangerous situations any number of times. But the seal was in his right hand, and he could not risk a proper fight while he held it. If it was damaged, everything that had happened, the entire war, would have all been for nothing.

"If you shoot me," said Gordon, "I'll drop the seal. You won't be able to catch it. It will smash on the flagstones, and there will be an end to my father's empire for us both." He took a careful step forward. "Let me see to Veronica."

Sark shook his head. "The seal. Give me the seal."

"No."

Suddenly, Sark spun around. Veronica lay slumped and bleeding in a pile of books; she was conscious, but only just, and her dark eyes were fixed on Gordon. Sark pointed the gun straight at her head.

"Give me the seal," he said, "or I'll shoot her."

Gordon stopped abruptly. His mouth went dry. He and Veronica had always known that they might be killed in battle. On several occasions, they nearly had been. But against the odds they had survived. Veronica had stuck by him, fought for him, believed in him when he no longer believed in himself. And now . . . Something black and horrible and enveloping came rushing up from deep within Gordon's heart. It was like being stifled in long lengths of black plastic so that he could not see, hear, breathe, or even move. Gordon knew without a shadow of doubt that Sark meant what he said. He would shoot Veronica without hesitation or compunction. If necessary, he would kill the rest of them as well to get what he wanted. And Gordon was going to let him do it. To keep the seal, he was going to let Veronica die.

The gun was pointed at Veronica's head. The seal grew hot against Gordon's palm. He loved Veronica. In all his life, he had never loved anybody more. But the seal was his inheritance. It had come to him like a promise from his father and he would not give it up. He loved Veronica. The seal was no use to Sark, but he would do anything to stop Gordon from keeping it. He loved her, loved her, loved her.... A tiny chink opened up in the blackness that surrounded him, and suddenly, for all the wrong reasons, he shouted at the top of his lungs, "*No!* I will not give you the seal! I will not give it up! I will not hand it over! *I am the Black Count!*"

Gordon lifted his hand. For an instant the full weight of the seal came down upon him and made him stagger. He saw Sark's hand jerk up, his look of alarm, and then some strength that was not his own took hold of him. His arm went back, and he hurled the seal at the wall.

The breath burst out of him. He hit the floor as if struck by a cannon. Gordon heard the gun go off and heard yells and crashes as Mr. Hartley and Sark's companions overpowered the general. A piece of plaster came down from the ceiling and smashed onto the flagstones near his head. The seal lay broken beside it in a thousand pieces, but Gordon was aware of nothing but the fact that Veronica was still alive.

Perhaps, thought Gordon, he had not done it for the wrong reason after all.

On the castle ramparts, cut off from the tower, King Lionel and Queen Evangeline perched on a crumbling pinnacle of masonry. Flame surrounded them, not green flame now, but ordinary fire from a fallen bomb. The steps down to the bailey were destroyed, and there was no way out. Evangeline was frantically slitting sandbags with a bayonet and throwing the sand on the flames. Lionel had tied a handkerchief around his mouth and was beating uselessly at the flames with an empty sack.

"It's no good, Evie. I can't—"

"Lionel! Look!" Choking and spluttering, Evangeline staggered to the battlements. Lionel followed her pointing finger. In the streets below, Gordon's soldiers were running away from the castle in panic, back to the fields where the army had camped. Lionel blinked. For a moment he couldn't believe what his weary, smoke-reddened eyes were seeing. All around the ramparts, exhausted cheers were going up, guns and Quenching Machines were fired into the air, the royal emblems were waved, and the great white-and-gold flag of Ashby flapped back and forth as the defenders who had saved it from the burning tower flung it over the walls and let it fly.

Evangeline whooped with joy and fell into her husband's arms.

"They're retreating!"

"Yes!" Lionel ripped the handkerchief elatedly from his mouth. The day was theirs. Even if he and Evangeline did not live to understand how the tide of battle had turned, he at least knew now that his kingdom would be safe. The flames flared up around him, and as he felt their scorching heat a giant flying shadow swooped overhead.

"Queen Dragon!" cried Evangeline.

"That's not Queen Dragon," said Lionel. "It's the wrong color—"

His words were cut off. The dragon dived toward the castle. Lionel saw its front claw swing down and then, so deftly it was like being tumbled onto a feather mattress, he and the queen were rolled up inside it and winging to safety.

"Ashby forever!" shouted Lily on King Dragon's head.

She lifted her fist and shook it in triumph. The baby princess gurgled with delight, and King Dragon opened his mouth. A roar of flame and smoke lit up the night sky from one end of Ashby Water to the other. In the fields Gordon's army of exhausted Black Squads and half-trained miners turned and fled into Ashby Thicket. Down King

Dragon swooped, scattering their ranks. A few of the braver ones tried to fire at them, but the rest simply ran for their lives. Lily let them go. She was interested in only one person, and as King Dragon turned and came flying back, she saw her. A hunched-up, ragged figure was darting from a tent. Lily reached into her fireproof cape and pulled out a syringelike object.

"Aunt Cassy!" she yelled. "This is for Annacondia!"

Lily aimed and depressed the plunger. A stream of Quenching Drops, crystal clear as the first snow to melt in the Black Mountains, arced out through the darkness toward the fleeing figure. At the last moment, Cassy turned. The Quenching Drops hit the vial of dragon's blood around her neck, and she screamed in rage. Smoke went pouring up from the vial, the chain holding it in place dissolved, and with an unexpected bang it fell to the ground and shattered.

Screaming and hissing, Aunt Cassy dodged and ran between the tents. She was fast, but King Dragon was quicker. He lunged down, his foot lashed out, and Cassy was trapped in the golden cage of his claws. This time, he was not so gentle. Lily could hear their captive howling and cursing in fury as they wheeled about and flew back in the direction of the castle. Seconds later, King Dragon soared over the broken walls and landed in the bailey amid a jumble of broken masonry and fallen sandbags.

The king and queen jumped out of one outstretched claw. Lily climbed down from King Dragon's head, more slowly than usual, for she was carrying the princess. When she saw Elizabeth, Queen Evangeline gave a choking cry and ran to gather her precious baby into her arms.

"Elizabeth!" Tears ran down Evangeline's smoke-stained face and as she buried her face in the princess's tiny shoulder, Lily felt her own eyes prickle with emotion. Meanwhile, in her dragon prison, Aunt Cassy was screaming and cursing and spitting at them.

"Keep your curses to yourself, you evil creature," said King Dragon sternly. "They cannot harm us, nor will we let you go free. You shall never harm anyone again, dragon or human."

"What are we going to do with her?" asked Lily.

"For now, we'll lock her up in the old dungeons," said Lionel. "There's plenty of space in the vaults."

"I don't think she'll be troubling us much longer," said Lily. "Aunt Cassy is thousands of years old. Without the dragon's blood she had in that vial, I am afraid she will die."

A door opened at the foot of the South Tower, and Mr. Hartley emerged, accompanied by a young man with dark hair. Lily looked at them curiously and wondered who the newcomer was. He looked familiar, but she did not recognize him; perhaps, since he was wearing a combat uniform, he was a prisoner. By now dawn was not far off, and a pale light began to reveal something of the destruction. The castle walls had been destroyed and blackened; the moat was choked with rubble; and fires still burned in the half-light, too fierce for the weary gangs of volunteers to bring under control. Mr. Hartley and his companion picked their way through the wreckage to where Lionel was standing. As Lily watched, the young man went down on his knees, took a knife from his belt, and handed it, hilt first, to the king. In that moment, Lily recognized him. It was Gordon.

"Your Majesty," he said. "I surrender. The day is yours."

chapter thirteen

The Last Chapter

It was late the following morning when Lily and King Dragon finally arrived at Queen Dragon's volcano. King Dragon had wanted to go immediately, but Lily was so exhausted she had fallen asleep against a pile of sandbags in the castle bailey, and they had not been able to leave Ashby Water until just after dawn. Luckily, King Dragon was much faster on the wing than Queen Dragon, and the long journey across the ocean was accomplished in what seemed to Lily like record time.

As they circled down into the volcano's crater, Lily spied Queen Dragon's crimson figure sitting on the shingle in front of the lake of boiling mud. Queen Dragon looked up at the sound of approaching wings and gave a cry of excitement. A moment later she and King Dragon were safely enfolded in each other's wings.

There were many tears, both human and dragon, and many explanations. At last, King Dragon stemmed the flow of Queen Dragon's talk and spoke his heart.

"Sinhault," he said, "a thousand years have passed in Eydelen since I saw you. I have mourned for Annacondia and I will never forget her. But I have also mourned for you, twice over. For centuries, a compulsion has been growing upon me to find you and bring you back to Eydelen. I want you to make your home there, to take the oath, to live among your fellow dragons in peace and prosperity until the end of your days."

"And that is really why you have come here?" said Queen Dragon wonderingly.

"Yes," said King Dragon. "But there is another

reason. If you are willing to have me, I think we should get married."

Queen Dragon burst into tears again. "I would marry you tomorrow," she wept. "I have waited for this moment all my life. But what about Lily? How could I leave her?"

"Lily is not a dragon," King Dragon admitted. "But she is, I think, the truest friend a dragon ever had. If she wishes it and it would make you happy, I see no reason why she should not come to Eydelen as well."

"Me? Live in Eydelen?" Lily was taken aback. "I—I wasn't expecting this."

"You don't have to make your mind up straightaway," King Dragon told her. "There is plenty of time to decide."

Lily shook her head. "For a dragon, perhaps there would be," she said. "But human beings only have a very short life, and we must spend it in the best way we can." She hesitated. It was not that she did not want to go to Eydelen. But things had changed so much that she could not begin to guess which direction her life would take if she stayed behind. Lily remembered what she had seen in the Pool of the Oracle in the Singing Wood, on her very first adventure with Queen Dragon. Like Eydelen, the Singing Wood was a place where time ran differently than in the rest of the world; there, she had been able to look into her own future. The grown-up Lily she had seen was beautiful and good, but there had been no Queen Dragon at her side. Suddenly, Lily realized that the end really had come. She would never again go to Skansey and sit beneath her apple trees on a spring morning. The sheep would graze on as they had always done, getting fat on the lush green grass; the ruins of her house would crumble until no one would even be able to tell it had been there. And across the straits, Queen Dragon's volcano would be empty. There would be plenty of work for Lily Quench, and many more adventures. But they were adventures she would experience alone.

"I cannot go to Eydelen," she said sadly. "It's not my home, Queen Dragon. I belong in Ashby with my human friends. If I went with you, I would only make both of us unhappy."

"Even in Eydelen?" asked Queen Dragon anxiously.

"Even in Eydelen," said Lily. "Don't forget, Queen Dragon. You were unhappy there yourself, for a little while."

"But what will you do?" persisted Queen Dragon.

"Grow up, I suppose," said Lily in a very small voice.

"Yes, I suppose you must," said Queen Dragon. She thought of something, and brightened. "On the other hand, if you cannot live with us, I see no reason why you should not come to visit."

Lily smiled through her tears. "I would like that, Queen Dragon. I would like it very much."

Queen Evangeline was washing Princess Elizabeth's nappies in a wooden tub and hanging them out to dry on the castle battlements when the flight of dragons appeared over the ocean. Even for someone who was accustomed to Queen Dragon's spectacular arrivals and departures, it was an amazing sight. Evangeline gasped, stepped backward, and kicked over her washtub. People stopped in the streets of Ashby Water and pointed upward. The castle servants, who were doing their best to clear the rubble from the courtyard, dropped the chunks of stone they were carrying and gawped like excited children. Seven dragons, all carrying chests of treasure, sailed over the castle in perfect formation. They bowed their heads politely as they passed, then swung around and landed, one after another, on the castle walls.

"Queen Evangeline of Ashby—my fiancé, King Dragon," said Queen Dragon proudly, as they landed near the queen and her washtub. King Dragon bowed politely in his golden magnificence. Evangeline bowed back. For the first time in her life, she couldn't help wishing she was dressed more like a real queen. Luckily, King Dragon didn't seem to notice her soapy arms and dirty sweater.

"With your permission, Your Majesty, we would like to get married here so Sinhault's human friends can be present," he said. "My companions and I are anxious to return to our own valley of Eydelen, so perhaps we could hold the ceremony tomorrow evening. I promise, there will be no trouble to yourselves."

"I'm sure there won't," said Evangeline. "A wedding's just what we need to cheer us up. Though, as a matter of fact, we've already had one today. Lily, Gordon and Veronica were married this morning in the Ashby Church."

"My goodness." Lily was taken aback. Adjusting to a grown-up Gordon was hard enough. It was even harder for her to imagine his being married.

"It was very quiet," said the queen. "Veronica's still quite weak, and, of course, they have no friends here. But at least Murdo was able to be there. He and Angela arrived back in Ashby Water this morning, in a dragonet."

"I can't imagine Murdo would have been very pleased," Lily remarked.

"He wasn't," said Evangeline. "He's been sulking ever since. But he'll get used to it. Now, Queen Dragon, King Dragon, is there anything I can do to help?"

King Dragon politely declined any further assistance, and the dragons set off to make their preparations. Lily went home to bed and slept soundly until the following morning. She spent the day at the castle helping with the cleanup, and though from time to time she saw dragons mysteriously flying overhead, there was no hint of what might await them later that day when the ceremony took place. Like a human bride,

Queen Dragon had withdrawn into her dragon house to make herself beautiful, and had not been seen since the day before. Though Lily would have loved to be there with her, neither she, nor even any female dragons had been invited. When she joined the other human guests in the Royal Procession from Ashby Castle, she had no idea at all what to expect.

King Lionel and Queen Evangeline led the way out through the gatehouse with Princess Elizabeth, followed by Gordon and Veronica, the Hartleys, Sir Wilibald Zouche, and Lily last of all. The wedding ceremony was to take place in the Ashby Botanic Garden, and as the party walked across the grass, the short winter day was already drawing to a close. Not far from the dragon house a mysterious round wooden structure had appeared overnight. Two young dragons, garlanded with gold and silver chains in the shape of flowers, stood waiting at the entrance to usher them in.

"My goodness!" Queen Evangeline looked up at the green branches waving overhead. A shower of damp pink petals flurried down in a gust of wind. "What on earth is this?"

"They're moon rose trees!" Lily stared at them

in delight. The dragons had uprooted entire moon rose trees from the forests in Eydelen and brought them to Ashby, where they had planted them in a circle and woven their branches into a kind of bower. The branches were covered with blossoms, and their scent filled the winter air like incense. Tiny lights burned everywhere in the branches, and as the guests walked through the opening in the trees they found themselves in a magical glade, as if they had been transported to another world.

Silken hangings from ancient castles floated from the branches, and huge piles of pink petals had been spread with coverlets for the human guests to sit on. Around the walls the dragons were already assembling, with more arriving all the time. At one end of the bower the trees had been woven together to form a bridal canopy, and in the center was an enormous bonfire, as yet unlit. But most amazing of all was Queen Dragon's bridal treasure. The chests, brought from her cavern under the volcano, had all been opened, and gold necklaces, crowns, silver belts, and corselets sparkled in the branches like so many Christmas decorations. The rest sat waiting, spread out upon the grass in preparation for the feast. In the flickering gaslight of Queen Dragon's cavern, Lily had always thought the treasure marvelous. Tonight, out in the open, it seemed incredible.

When everybody, human and dragon, had formed an expectant circle around the bonfire, a huge burst of flame lit up the sky. They all rose immediately to their feet as King Dragon soared overhead, flame streaming from his nostrils in triumphant bursts. He landed in the bower and as he took his place under the canopy, all the dragons began to sing. It was a remarkable sound, for every dragon was singing a different tune, but somehow it all fitted together.

Hail to you, Queen Dragon!
Hail, glorious bride.
Home to Eydelen we bring you,
King Dragon at your side!
Hail to you, Queen Dragon!
Hail, glorious bride!

As the words rose up into the darkening sky, Queen Dragon herself entered the bower. She came alone, through the opening left between the tree trunks, and as she passed across the grass to the bridal canopy, Lily thought she had never looked more beautiful. Her crimson scales gleamed, her eyes sparkled, and she looked so happy that as she passed, the entire congregation burst into spontaneous applause. When she reached the canopy, King Dragon stepped forward and they stood together, facing their guests. Then King Dragon reached out and took Queen Dragon's claw in his.

"Sinhault Fierdaze," he said solemnly. "Before this assembly of friends, I take you as my wife, on earth, in air, and in fire. For the rest of our days, my cave will be your cave, and we shall never be parted. To my last tooth, I will protect you. To my last scale, I will provide for you. All this I swear on blood and fire. May I be cast into the deepest sea if I ever forget this pledge."

"King Dragon, I accept your pledge," Queen Dragon answered. "Before this assembly of friends, I take you as my husband, on earth, in air, and in fire. With my blood I will love you. With my heart, I will comfort and protect you, and we shall never be parted. All this I swear on blood and fire. May I be cast into the deepest sea if I ever forget this oath."

As Queen Dragon's vows faded into the night

air, the two dragons flung back their heads. Twin streams of flame spurted and mingled from their nostrils, and the bonfire in front of them burst into joyful flames. The dragons in the assembly beat their wings, and the humans cheered and clapped. Queen Dragon and her new husband looked shyly at each other, then leaned together and entwined their necks in a kiss.

"And now," said King Dragon, "let the wedding feast begin!"

With whoops of joy, the young dragons descended on the treasure chests. Since the dragons were not used to catering for humans, Lily and her friends were not quite so well looked after, but there was certainly plenty of roast meat on the menu, and to compensate, they were presented with many of the more attractive bits of treasure to take away as souvenirs. There were speeches and toasts, which King Lionel proposed in ginger beer he had thoughtfully supplied, and several rather convoluted dragon jokes that the humans didn't get. Finally, two young dragons came flying overhead and showered the happy couple with gold coins.

It was all too wonderful to take in. As Lily

watched Queen Dragon standing at her husband's side, flushed with excitement and overcome with joy after thousands of years of separation and sadness, it seemed to her that there was hardly any point in saying good-bye. What was she, a small human girl, compared to such enormous love? In a thousand years' time, would Queen Dragon even remember her? A choking knot of emotion swelled in her throat, and since she knew she must not cry and ruin things, she slipped out through the doorway and hurried away.

Outside the bower it was cold and mercifully dark. Lily walked across the grass until she reached the dragon house and leaned up against its rough stone walls. In the darkness, alone, the tears she had been holding back came suddenly flowing down in torrents. She cried for herself, for Queen Dragon, for the time they had spent together, and for their parting. In a few moments she would be as alone as she had been on the dreadful day in the cemetery when her grandmother Ursula had been buried; the day Queen Dragon had come so unexpectedly into her life.

"Lily?" Lily looked up. Queen Dragon was standing in front of her. A few gold coins glittered where they had caught in her scales, but they were not so round or golden as the great kindly serpent eyes that now looked down upon her. Lily tried to look into them, but they were so filled with concern and love that the tears flowed up and choked her again and she had to turn away.

"Oh, Queen Dragon," she said. "I will miss you."

"And I, you," said Queen Dragon. She lowered her head and Lily turned to her. For a moment they stood together, Lily's tiny human face in its fireproof cape pressed up against Queen Dragon's crimson cheek, her little hands spread out against the enormous scales. It was the moment of good-bye, and both of them knew it. Yet in the same moment, Lily also knew that she had been wrong in thinking Queen Dragon would forget her. They had shared something special, and though it could not last forever, she, too, would remember Queen Dragon to the end of her days.

They turned at length and walked together back to the bower. As they passed beneath the entrance, Lily noticed that the moon rose trees were sprouting; they had dug their roots into the earth and new buds were forming and opening. It was a small miracle, and though Lily did not know whether or not the trees would survive the dragons' passing, she was grateful that, for this brief moment in time, some of Eydelen's magic had seeped out into her own world.

"Good-bye, Lily, my darling," said Queen Dragon softly.

Lily blinked and nodded. She looked up at the sky, and above the canopy of blossoming flowers, the winter stars seemed very bright through her tears. Queen Dragon took her place at King Dragon's side. Suddenly there was a rent in the air, and everything was full of light. The whole of Eydelen was opened up before them, and Lily realized that it was bigger than any of them had thought. There was a whirring of dragon wings, a flash of fire. Then the dragons were gone, and the sky was cold and empty and full of stars.

"Good-bye, Queen Dragon," whispered Lily. "I love you."

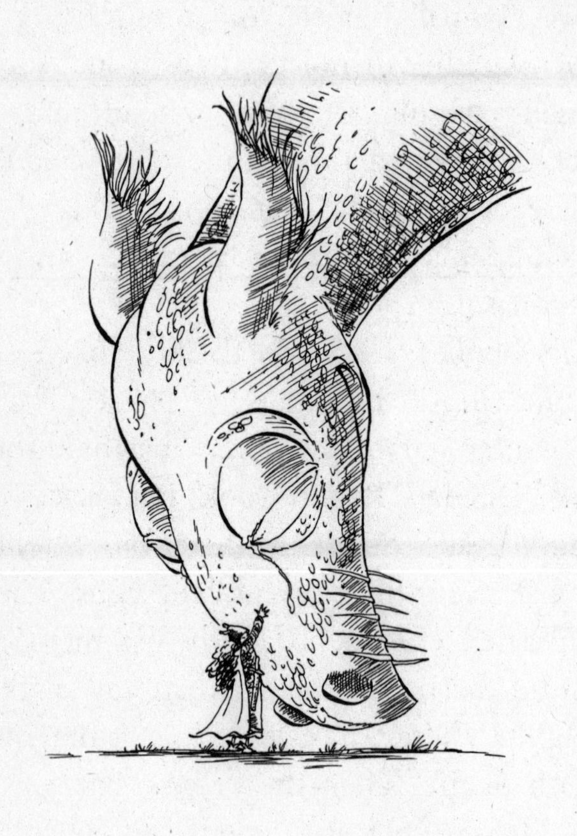

Don't Miss Lily's other exciting adventures. . . .

Lily Quench and the Dragon of Ashby

Meet Lily Quench as she embarks on her very first dragon-slaying mission—a mission with a most unexpected outcome!

Lily Quench and the Black Mountains

Lily and her friend Queen Dragon embark on a perilous journey to the Black Mountains where they must find the magical blue lily: the only thing that can save the town of Ashby Water.

Lily Quench and the Treasure of Mote Ely

Kidnapped and taken back into the past to a crumbling castle in the middle of a creepy marsh, Lily Quench searches for the long-lost treasure of Mote Ely—and a way back to her own time.

Lily Quench and the Lighthouse of Skellig Mor

Faced with her greatest challenge yet, Lily must release deadly sea dragons, find Queen Dragon, and discover the secret to the Eyes in Time so that she can save her homeland and her friends.

Lily Quench and the Magicians' Pyramid

Armed with the secret to the Eyes in Time, Lily sets out once again to find the creators of these magical—and dangerous—devices.

Lily Quench and the Hand of Manuelo

Lily Quench goes in search of an elusive hero known only as Manuelo to find out exactly who he is and why he's causing the miners to revolt against the Black Empire.